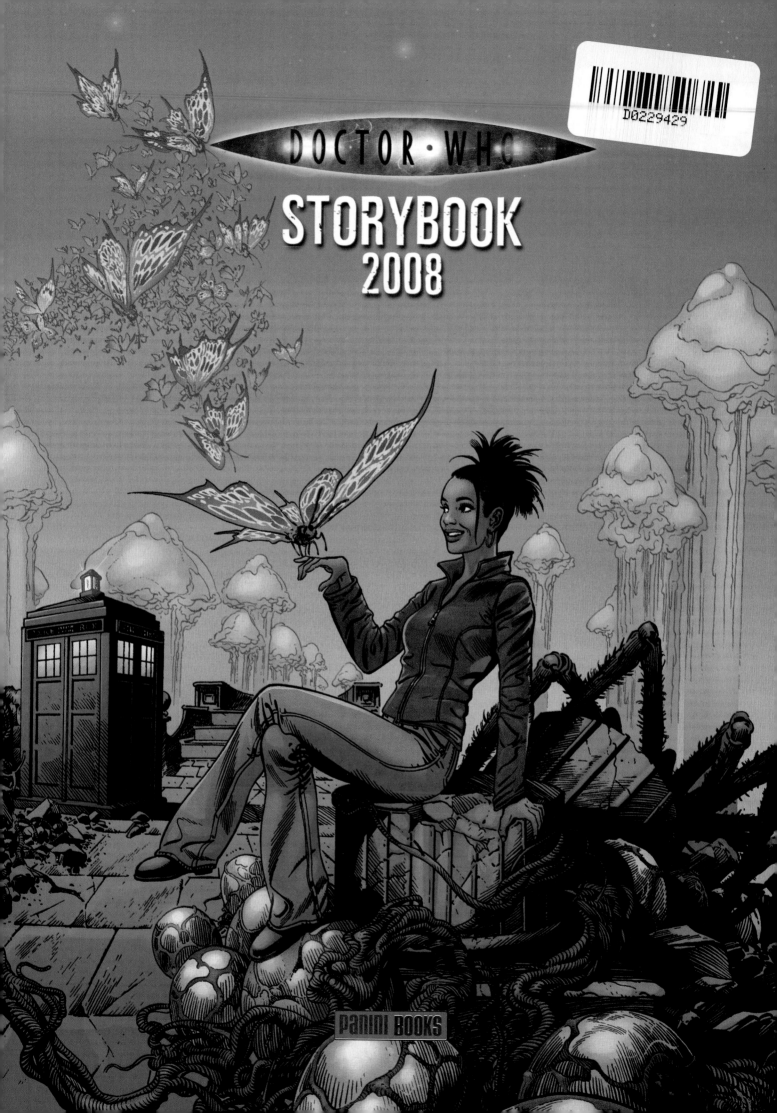

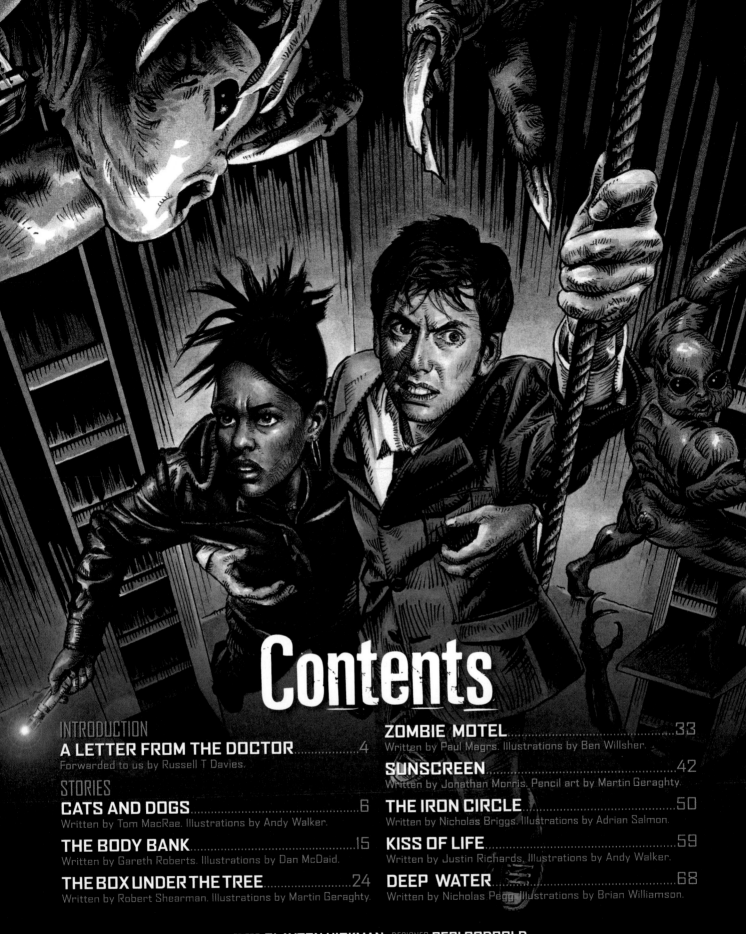

Contents

EDITOR **CLAYTON HICKMAN** DESIGNER **PERI GODBOLD**

FRONT COVER PAINTING BY **ALISTER PEARSON**

FRONTISPIECE PENCILS & INKS BY **DAVID A ROACH** FRONTISPIECE COLOURS BY **DYLAN TEAGUE** CONTENTS PAGE ILLUSTRATION BY **ANDY WALKER**

WITH THANKS TO **RUSSELL T DAVIES, DAVID TENNANT & FREEMA AGYEMAN, MARK GATISS, GARY RUSSELL, TOM SPILSBURY, SCOTT GRAY, STUART MANNING, KATE BEHARRELL, RICHARD HOLLIS** & **HARRIET NEWBY-HILL**

A letter from the Doctor

The Ice-Swamps of Mallarg,
Mallargshire,
Mallarg,
Galaxy 7.

Mayvember the fruth.

Hello all!

For once I've been taking it easy. Yeah, Martha and me, we fancied a quick holiday on Mallarg. It turned out to be very quick because after a full two minutes lying on our loungers outside the TARDIS, the Ice Swamps came to life and started chasing us. You see, it really is worth getting the most up-to-date guidebooks before you set off on your break, just to see if anything's changed. Perhaps that famous restaurant has reopened as a nightclub, or early closing is now Wednesday not Thursday, or the frozen slime has evolved into a monster with a taste for flesh.

Anyway, during my two minutes of holiday fun I got through some holiday reading. All of them classics: Dickens' 'Great Expectations', Tolstoy's 'War And Peace', Kinsella's 'Shopaholic Ties The Knot'. I laughed, I cried, I couldn't put them down. No really, I really couldn't put them down, thanks to the quanta-meg-magnetism effect of Mallarg's sun.

But I saved the best til last, with this very volume you now hold in your hands. Here are some of our adventures that you'll never see on television: the motel haunted by zombies; the boy who found the TARDIS under his Christmas tree; the cats and dogs who learned to talk; the woman chased by a giant bionic tortoise; the electricity pylons that came to life. Yeah. Maybe that's why you won't see them on television...

I'd just finished this Storybook when Martha tugged my arm and pointed out that the ice swamp was trying to eat us. I hope nothing similar happens to you before, during or after you read it. And if it does, stand absolutely still. No, not really, RUN! Like I'm doing now. Yes, I can type a letter while I'm running, thank you very much. You'd be surprised the things I can do while I'm running.

Happy times and places,

The Doctor

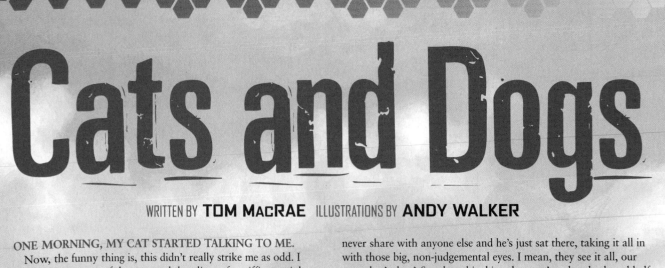

Cats and Dogs

WRITTEN BY **TOM MacRAE**   ILLUSTRATIONS BY **ANDY WALKER**

ONE MORNING, MY CAT STARTED TALKING TO ME.

Now, the funny thing is, this didn't really strike me as odd. I mean, I'm not one of those crystal-dangling tofu-sniffing nutjobs who thinks animals are all secretly tuned into their own special language and that if we could only free ourselves from the shackles of the capitalist Western mindset then we'd be open to their truth, and I don't want to be Doctor Doolittle either (The Rex Harrison Doctor Doolittle I mean – no-one wants to be Eddie Murphy). It's not that I ever expected it to happen, it's just that, when it did, it didn't seem that weird. I mean, the note-to-self, <u>that</u> was weird. But this – well, some things you just take in your stride.

I mean, I know for a fact my cat can't talk. That's why he's so great to talk *to*. Not because he understands me, but because he doesn't understand anything, and because he doesn't understand anything, you can tell him everything. And he's seen me naked, or having a poo, or naked never share with anyone else and he's just sat there, taking it all in with those big, non-judgemental eyes. I mean, they see it all, our pets, don't they? So when this thing that you've already shared half your life with suddenly takes the extra step of jumping up onto your bed at 7am and wishing you "Good morning" then it's just... well, it's *odd*, don't get me wrong – really, really odd. Just not that surprising.

"Good morning," said my cat, sitting on my bed, looking up at me like this was all perfectly normal. I stared at him for about a minute then decided I wasn't dreaming.

"I'm sorry," I said, "but would you mind repeating that?"

"Of course not," said Biggles politely. "Good morning."

I stared at him a for a bit longer.

"You couldn't do that yesterday," I said finally.

"No," said Biggles, nodding sagely at my wise observation. There was another uncomfortable pause, which Biggles filled by licking his bum. I was racking my brain for an explanation, because I didn't want to seem thick by having to ask my cat how this was all happening. I felt it this out for myself. I mean, it was like needing a pet to explain to you how to open their tin of pet food. It makes you feel all devolved.

So, I sat in bed looking round, trying to avoid Biggles' gaze and thinking and thinking and thinking about how you get a talking cat, until my eyes fell on my wardrobe and with a flash of inspiration I suddenly blurted out:

"Narnia!"

Biggles rolled his eyes, sighed patiently and said "No. Not Narnia."

"Okay then," I said. "Tell me how you're doing it. Speaking I mean. Not licking your bum."

"After breakfast," said Biggles, jumping down and running out the room.

MY NOTE-TO-SELF WAS STILL SITTING THERE ON THE microwave. I'd written it a while ago to be read later on, except I could never remember what I'd written or why I'd written it. It was folded in half and on the front I'd put 'TO BE OPENED IN TIME'. Why I'd written that I don't have a clue, but it didn't seem to be time yet so I hadn't looked inside, and so the note had just sat there for a week or two, unopened and ignored. I was thinking that this was probably not normal

behaviour as I rooted round through the pet food cupboard.

"Do you still like the tuna one?" I asked Biggles, getting a tin down.

"If I'm honest," he said, "I've never been a fan."

"You ate that frog that got run over flat and dried out in the sun." I said. "Now's not the time to get fussy." But I put the tuna one back and got out a chicken supreme instead.

Biggles asked me; "You know those really expensive pet foods, in the little pouches with all fresh pasta and peas and stuff in them?"

"Yeah?"

"Waste of money. We don't care. I mean – pasta? What's that about? We're cats, not Italians."

"Ooh, actually," I said, thinking out loud, "I've always wanted to ask you – do you actually eat mice or is that just in cartoons?"

"I've been known to snack, yes."

"Okay, so, don't you reckon mouse flavour cat food would sell? Only it's such an obvious idea and no-one's done it."

Biggles considered this.

"Where would you get the mice from? That's the flaw in your plan. I don't think you can farm them."

"Someone must. You get them in pet shops."

"I don't know. Look it up on Wikipedia."

A couple of joggers ran past the front window, and it suddenly occurred me that they had probably not spent the morning in conversation with their pets.

"Why?"

"Apparently, the universe ends if you say it. Or something."

"What is he then, God?"

Biggles considered this.

"No," he eventually offered. "God shouldn't be that irritating."

"Well, where does the Doctor live?"

"Nowhere. Everywhere. He just travels round."

"Like a district nurse?" I said. "Why's he so important anyway?"

"I need something sorted out, and he's a bit of a fixer."

"Like what? I mean, not to be rude, but you're a cat. It's not like you've had a tough week at the office, is it?"

"I've got family responsibilitie,s" countered Biggles, a bit annoyed.

"Ohhh!" I said, grinning like a fool. "You're a dad!"

"Yes, but that's not the point. The point is, I am a talking cat, and I need to speak to the Doctor, and if that seems odd, then I'd remind you of the start of this sentence where I said 'I am a talking cat'"

I nodded. "In context," I said, "nothing seems truly odd any more."

"Will you help me though?"

"Of course. What do you want me to do?"

Ten minutes later Biggles and I were hunched over my computer, doing an internet search on 'the Doctor' 'police box' and 'recent sightings'. It turned out that Biggles was a lot more computer savvy than me, but had incompatibility issues with paws and a qwerty keyboard. Basically, I was there to do the typing.

Quite a few pages flashed up, although why anyone was interested in a police box (if I'm honest, I'm not sure what that is anyway) was beyond me. Biggles seemed very interested in all this though, and said he could see a pattern in the Doctor's appearances.

The phone rang and I left Biggles to read through the pages on his own. The caller was Mary, my next door neighbour. Mary retired about ten years ago and was pretty independent, but I always did her shopping for her. She had this little poodle called Sampson who was one of Biggles's perennial enemies, although I thought he was sweet and, for a dog, didn't smell too bad.

"Hello Mary," I said, wondering if she'd run out of tea bags again. "How are you?"

"Well, dear," she replied, "in myself, I'm fine, but I think there's something queer with Sampson."

"Oh dear," I said. "What's the matter with him?"

"I'm not sure what the proper technical term would be, but he seems to have started talking."

FIVE MINUTES LATER I WAS SITTING IN MARY'S LOUNGE with a plate of bourbon creams on my lap. I decided not to tell Biggles about Sampson also finding his voice all of a sudden. They'd been bad enough scrapping with each other when they were dumb animals. The thought of them getting into a verbal slanging match as well was too much at the moment. Besides, Biggles seemed absorbed with the computer at the moment after working

"Oh God," I said. "I've gone mad."

"Nope. Promise you. This is all really happening."

I looked at Biggles, and something in his eyes seemed vaguely reassuring.

"Promise?"

"Promise."

"And it's really you?"

"Of course. Ask me anything."

"Okay. When I first got you when you were a little kitten, what did I call you?"

"Dolly. Then you had to change my name when you realised I wasn't a girl."

"Wow," I said. "You really are the talking version of you."

"Listen," said Biggles. "Can I ask you a favour?"

"Of course."

"I need to contact someone. It's really important."

"Ok. Who?"

"He's called the Doctor."

Contacting the Doctor wasn't as easy as you might first imagine. For starters, it turned out he wasn't an actual Doctor – like a medical one – so he wasn't in the phone book or contactable through NHS direct, and what's more he didn't seem to have any actual name.

"Just 'the Doctor'," said Biggles. "No-one knows his real name."

out that he could type with his tail.

Mary was in her kitchen but I could hear the sound of her voice floating through the door.

"Sampson!" she called, "Get down off the table you naughty, naughty dog!"

"Mary," Sampson replied in measured tones, "I have explained to you already; I need to be up here to get my work done. I am not a naughty dog, I'm just on a tight schedule."

There was something peculiar about hearing Sampson answer her back. Mary, despite accepting that Sampson could now speak, didn't seem to find it necessary to treat him any differently than she had when he was a dumb dog.

"Well it's time for your wee. Are you going on your own or do you want me to walk you?"

"Oh God, Mary," said Sampson, "you're so embarrassing."

I realised there was something in my pocket. It was my note-to-self, with TO BE OPENED IN TIME still written on the front. That was odd, because I didn't remember picking it up, but I suppose I must have done for it to be there. But it didn't seem time to open it yet, so I put it back in my jacket.

Mary came in with a cup of tea for me.

"I'm not sure about this talking business – it's like having a man in the house again, and that was bad enough the first time round."

"I *can* hear you, you know," called Sampson.

Mary rolled her eyes and mouthed 'ignore him' at me, and it hit me that they really did seem like an old married couple.

"Hello Sampson," I called to the kitchen. He trotted to the open door and peered at me.

"You never said we had company Mary," he said.

"Well," replied Mary, "I can't say I'd ever felt the need to ask your permission before."

Sampson nodded and trotted away again.

"When did this start?" I asked Mary.

"This morning. I don't know what brought it on, unless – do you think it could be that new pet food?"

I assured Mary that it probably wasn't.

"Still," she said, "it is queer."

There was a crashing sound from the kitchen.

"Are you up on my table again?" shouted Mary.

"Mind your own business," replied Sampson.

"What's he doing in there?" I asked.

"Pulling my old radio apart from the looks of it, though he calls it a making a 'communications device' – but who's a dog going to communicate with, I ask you? I think he's ill you know. He keeps asking for a doctor."

"A doctor?" I asked. "Or *the* Doctor?"

Mary thought on this.

"The Doctor," she replied. "Definitely *the* Doctor."

ON THE SHORT WALK BACK TO MY HOUSE, I realised there were a lot more cats around than you'd normally find. In fact, there were hundreds, if not thousands, and most of them were sitting in my front garden or perching on the window sills and ledges at the front of my house. They stared at me as I went up to my door, and although none of them spoke I could see the intelligence in their eyes; these were talking cats.

Biggles looked annoyed with me when I came in.

"And where have *you* been?" he asked curtly.

"Next door," I answered. "Uh, there's a lot of cats outside…"

"They're with me. I've been unable to track the Doctor down precisely, but my research would indicate that he's somewhere in this general area. There's even been a direct sighting of the TARDIS, just up the street."

"The whatdis?"

"Never mind. If we can just get hold of him
– speak to him. Then he can sort this mess out."

"What mess, Biggles?" I asked, peering out the window at the
masses of cats outside.

"There was a treaty, an unjust prohibition, and now this
dimensional glitch – it's not fair, we were *so* close."

I stared at Biggles for quite a while as things started to fall into
place in my head.

"You're not my cat, are you?" I asked

"Yes and no," Biggles replied. "But mostly no."

"Where is he?"

"Inside this body, sharing it with me. Don't worry. I'll give him
back to you once I go."

"Go where?"

"Home. If we can find the Doctor. Do you know how long I've
been stuck in this body? Two weeks. Fourteen days that is. Three
hundred and thirty six long hours trying to work out how to get
these primitive vocal chords to support speech. And a cat's mind!
It's a jumble of rubbish – so un-evolved. It was impossible to
access Biggles's actual memories. Cat mind patterns are completely
untranslatable."

"Then how did you know about me calling you Dolly?"

"I read your mind, filled in the gaps with your own memories."

"You can do that? Wow. What am I thinking now?"

"A blue goldfish, Anthea Turner and the letter T."

I gasped. He was spot on. My fingers brushed against the note-to-
self in my pocket, and I put it back on top of the microwave without
really thinking.

"And Biggles is alright?"

"Yes. I have done this before you know – a trans-species body
possession. Species 29s are very good at it. That's the name of my

race. Species 29."

"Don't you have a proper name?"

"That *is* a proper name. I'm from a planet where
everything is very neatly categorised. It makes things much easier to
manage. If it wasn't for those wretched Species 7s."

"Who are they?"

"The 7s and the 29s have been at war for years. Or at
least, we try to be. If it wasn't for The Ageless and their damn
interventionism."

I was about to ask more, when the sound of barking came from
outside. Biggles and I looked out the window. As many dogs as there
were cats outside my house had gathered around Mary's lawn. More
were trotting down the street to join them.

"That's a lot of dogs," mused Biggles.

"Yeah," I said. "I don't know if I should tell you this, but
Sampson – Mary's poodle – he's started speaking too."

Biggles's fur stood up on end as he spun to stare at me.

"Dogs!" he hissed. "I should have guessed! Typical of them
– they're such cheats!"

"Who are?"

"Species 7s!"

Apparently, I was now involved in a high level diplomatic
conference. To the uninitiated, it would have looked as if I was
simply taking tea with Mary in her living room with our respective
pets sat beside us. In fact, Biggles and Sampson were negotiating for
the future of their respective species.

Biggles had demanded that I take him at once to Mary's house
(hiding him in my old rucksack so that we could get past the dogs
sat outside) and had then revealed himself to Sampson with a great
flourish once we got indoors.

"Species 7, I presume?" hissed Biggles, leaping out my rucksack.

"Species 29! What a surprise," Sampson had rejoindered.

"And this is Mary," I reminded Biggles. "It's her house, so be nice."

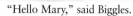

"Hello Mary," said Biggles.

"Hello Biggles," said Mary.

"I take it you've been trying to contact the Doctor?" said Biggles, looking at the mess of spare parts in the kitchen. "Any luck?"

"No." Said Sampson. "You?"

"Unfortunately not. Although there have been sightings nearby."

"So I heard," said Sampson. "But all reports of his activity ceased two weeks ago. As if he went to ground."

"Two weeks… That *is* interesting. I've been in this body and on this world for two weeks."

"As have I," said Sampson, scratching his chin with his back leg.

"So you say," said Biggles contemptuously. "But who can trust a Species 7? You probably arranged all this yourself. Trapping me and my people in the bodies of domestic cats!"

"No!" barked Sampson. "Such treachery and underhandedness is the mark of the true Species 29! It is clear to myself and all my canine brethren that *you* trapped *us* in these useless dogbodies!"

"Excuse me," I said, interrupting. "Do I take it from this that both your species are trapped in animal bodies?"

"Yes," said Biggles and Sampson simultaneously.

"Then isn't it likely that you're both victims of the same circumstance. I mean, neither of you has anything to gain from being like this."

Sampson and Biggles considered this.

"The human is correct," said Sampson. "Perhaps neither species is responsible for our current predicament."

Mary raised her hand.

"Can I ask what's going on?" she said. "Only I've been ever so patient, staying quiet and trying to follow as best I can, but I'm completely vexed now."

"Very well," said Sampson, "I suppose I owe you that much. You have tickled my belly very pleasantly these last two weeks after all. I shall tell you the truth."

I sat forward in my chair, ready to hear this, and realised to my surprise that my note-to-self had somehow found its way back into my pocket and there was something new next to it – a sort of small tube thing that I was sure wasn't mine. But I wasn't worried about notes or tubes at the moment; I wanted to hear the story of Species 7 and Species 29.

"In the beginning," began Sampson,

"I think we can skip forward a few millennia," yawned Biggles. Sampson huffed, but agreed.

"Very well," he said. "Let's start with the War."

THE STORY WENT SOMETHING LIKE THIS: THERE WERE many different species upon the homeworld, but none more warlike than Species 7 and Species 29. These two troublesome races had been involved with one of the greatest wars seen in their galaxy, which at one point threatened to wipe out the entire universe. Rather than let that happen, a neutral group from a neighbouring galaxy called The Ageless decided to intervene. They stopped the war with their superior technology, then put sanctions in place to prevent it from ever starting again.

"It was terrible," explained Biggles. "They banned us from ever owning physical bodies again."

I had to get him to repeat that bit, as it took a bit of getting used to.

"They banned us from having bodies – separated our conscious minds from the physical world. That way we couldn't fight a war. We had nothing to fight it with."

"Okay," I said, shrugging. "I'll believe anything today."

Apparently, after Species 29 and Species 7 were forbidden from owning bodies, they lived in peace for a thousand years, and as they were so well behaved, The Ageless decided to review their punishment. They arranged a great conference between the

disembodied essences of Species 29 and Species 7 to see if they had learned their lesson and deserved their bodies back. An impartial observer had to be appointed to oversee proceedings and make the final judgement on whether the two species should have their physical forms returned. The Ageless nominated the Doctor, who apparently was good at sticking his nose into that sort of thing. The final decision as to whether Species 7 and Species 29 would get their bodies back rested with him.

"But before the Doctor could arrive to start the hearing," Biggles explained, "some dimensional rift thing suddenly opened in the middle of the council chamber. We were all sucked into it. Next thing I knew, I was playing with a ball of string."

"And I was chasing my tail," added Sampson. "Which, two weeks on, continues to elude me."

"You mean," said Mary, "your spirits – or whatever you call them – got shoved into the bodies of our pets? Like stuffing in a turkey?"

"Yes," said Biggles and Sampson together, licking their lips at the analogy.

"Let me get this straight," I said, putting it all together. "Two of the most lethally warlike alien species of all time got reborn on our world, one side as cats, the other as dogs?"

"Indeed," said Biggles. "The irony has not escaped us."

"And now we need to go home," said Sampson, "and complete the negotiations in order to have our bodies returned to us."

"So that you can live in peace." I added.

"No!" cried Sampson and Biggles together. "To renew our beautiful war!"

"What?" I cried. "Are you mad? A thousand years of peace and you want to throw it away?!"

"We *love* war!" yelled Biggles. "We were born to battle! It is in our nature, in our blood, written in the core of our very DNA! Without war we are nothing! War is all!"

"But what about the rest of the universe! You nearly wiped us out last time!"

"Such is the price of war!" hissed Biggles, getting very excited and jumping up onto an occasional table. I think he forgot for a moment that he couldn't stand on two legs and nearly fell off it again as he tried to emphasise his impassioned speech with hand gestures.

"You," said Mary to Sampson, "are a bad dog. Get in your basket. Go on! In your basket!"

Sampson ignored Mary and started barking at Biggles, trying (unsuccessfully) to jump up on the occasional table after him.

"The Doctor has abandoned us!" woofed Sampson. "Let us bring our war to Earth!"

"Yes!" cried Biggles. "We shall wreak beautiful chaos here!"

"You're just cats and dogs!" I shouted at them. "Have some perspective!"

"Not *just* cats and dogs!" howled Biggles. "Super-intelligent, hyper-evolved, *psychic* cats and dogs! And we shall war! War! War!"

"War! War! War!" joined in Sampson, and from outside came the screeching and barking of a thousand cats and a thousand dogs replying in unison; "War! War! War!"

Mary and I took a step closer together and Biggles leaped out an open window, Sampson close on his heels. We rushed to the window, and looked out on a scene of chaos. All we could see were cats and dogs. There must have been close on a million of them now, sitting in trees, on cars, under hedges, clogging the road and surrounding mine and Mary's houses. The cats were on one side of the battlefield, the dogs on the other and at the moment neither side was advancing. They just stood their ground and howled at each other, but any moment – you could feel it in the air – all hell was going to break loose.

"I'm glad you're here," said Mary, gripping my hand, "even though I haven't known you very long."

"What do you mean?" I asked. "I've lived next door for years."

"No, dear. You moved in two weeks ago."

I looked at her, surprised. I was absolutely sure I hadn't, but when she said it, something sort of *tweaked* in my head, like an older, truer memory had popped to the surface, and I wondered if she might be right.

"Two weeks?" I said. "That's cropping up a lot, isn't it? I wonder what happened two weeks ago to start all this?"

"Never mind two weeks – what are we going to do now?!"

I realised that my note-to-self and the tube thing had somehow found themselves into my hands, even though I didn't remember taking them out my pocket. I looked at the note. TO BE OPENED IN TIME. I looked out the window at the massing forces of cat and dog, like some apocalyptic *Tom & Jerry* cartoon waiting to happen. I suddenly realised it was time.

"You know what I'm going to do Mary?" I said. "I'm going to read my note."

I opened the note. Inside were four words. Just four. But they changed everything. The note said:

'You are the Doctor'.

And I suddenly remembered. Yes I was.

"RIGHT," I YELLED, GRABBING THE TUBE thing which of course I now knew was my sonic screwdriver. "You can stop all that, right now!" and I set the screwdriver to deliver a powerful sonic blast across the street which was inaudible to humans but painfully audible to cats and dogs. And Time Lords for that matter. Ringing headache. Ouch. But you can't put a price on a good entrance.

I rushed outside, coat flapping, pushing through the throngs of disorientated cats and dogs until I found Biggles and Sampson, at the helm of their respective forces.

"Species 29 and Species 7 – will you never learn?" I cried, striking a dramatic pose. "Here you are, best strategic brains in the galaxy, and you waste it all on your pointless, never-ending war. I'd be cross with you, I really would, if you didn't look so darned cute. Yes you do. Look at you. Yes you do."

"Who are you?" demanded Biggles, recoiling from my chin-tickling.

"Oh, sorry," I said. "I'm the Doctor. Nice to meet you properly."

"The Doctor? You're not the Doctor. You don't look like the Doctor!"

"Well, there were these Daleks and the heart of the TARDIS and this frankly epic kiss and – well, long story. But I'm the real deal alright and do you know what?"

Biggles and Sampson stared at me.

"What?" asked Biggles.

"You've been a very naughty boy."

Biggles went to say something back to me, but I'd had enough of listening and decided to launch into a really brilliant speech, which I am fantastically good at making.

"So here's the problem. The Ageless – nice bunch by the way, fantastic artists, did you know they've just invented an extra colour? It's called frume. How brilliant is that? So anyway, The Ageless ask me, as a favour, if I can decide whether you 27s and 9s have really given up your violent ways for good or if you're just faking it to get your bodies back and kick off again on the sly. 'Well' I think, 'how can I, brilliant as I am – and I am brilliant – work that one out when you lot are renowned for being the best liars in the galaxy, after the Sisters Of Falsehood, the Deceivions from planet Fibb and Jeffrey Archer? So I came up with this idea – brilliant idea – I'll arrange a little 'accident', a little transdimensional quirk that'll give you physical bodies again. Not your original bodies you understand – that'd be too dangerous, but a nice safe set of arms and legs for you to test-drive, see what happens. Well, I say 'arms and legs', actually it was more –"

"Paws and tails!" interrupted Sampson.

"Give the dog a bone!" I shouted, patting him on the head. "Cats and dogs. Exactly. What better way to see if you'd given up your warring ways? Stick your essences in the form of nature's perennial enemies. Then sit back and see what you get up to."

I gestured at the armies of cats and dogs.

"And look what you got up to." I said, with a sad shake of the head. "You haven't learned, have you, and I gave you every opportunity. Got myself a house and a cat, called it Biggles (the cat that is, not the house, that'd be silly) just so the leader of Species 29 had a body to inhabit. I even made sure the neighbour

had a dog so the leader of Species 7 had a body to inhabit. Then you see, I could keep it all close to home, keep a proper eye on you. And – and this really shows what a pro I am – I even went so far as to temporarily restructure my own memories so that you couldn't read my mind and see through me, leaving only a paper note as a mental trigger to reinstate my proper self. Actually, thinking about that, in hindsight, that was a bit risky wasn't it? Could have dropped it by mistake. Could have blown away in a freak gust. Imagine that. World War 3 on planet Earth, all because of a dodgy filing system."

"What will you do now?" asked Biggles, trembling a bit.

"Give The Ageless my verdict. It probably won't surprise you to know that I'll be recommending they don't lift the ban on you owning bodies. In fact, that'll be them now," I said, pointing up as a shadow fell across the street.

Hanging in the sky above us was The Ageless diplomatic ship. Beautiful thing. Like a conch shell at a disco. Gotta love that Ageless style. Mind you, takes them an eternity to get ready to go out in the evening. Probably that's why they ended up immortal. They'd never find time to get anything done otherwise.

"Curse you Doctor!" yelled Biggles (like I'd never heard that before). "This shall not stop us!"

"Um, well…" I said, pretty sure that it would. The Ageless ship released a burst of transdimensional matter restorative, bathing the street in bright light. The true essences of the Species 29s and Species 7s were being sucked out of the cats and dogs.

"No!" continued Biggles. "You have not heard the last of Species 29!" (like I'd never heard that before either).

"We shall have our war! We shall have our revenge! We shall have our meow, meow, meow, purr, purr, meow." Finished Biggles, as the essence of the leader of Species 29 was finally liberated from its borrowed body. Then he sat down in the street and started giving his bum a good lick.

"Funny," I thought. "That's how it all started."

I gave The Ageless diplomatic ship a wave as it zipped back up into the stratosphere, and shooed the un-possessed cats and dogs to start making their way home.

"Is he alright?" asked Mary, looking at Sampson.

"Absolutely, one hundred percent back to normal." I replied, giving him a quick sonic scan just to be sure. "Ready to go home."

"Well, that's a relief."

"Hey, Mary," I said, getting an idea. "Do you fancy a cat too?"

SO THERE ENDS THE STORY OF BIGGLES AND SAMPSON (who went to live with Mary) and Species 27 and Species 9, (who returned to a disembodied but peaceful existence on their own homeworld). As for me, I packed up the few things I had in the house that been home for two weeks, marvelled at how humans ever get so attached to such unexciting, immobile properties which are the same size on the inside as on the outside, and locked the back door for the final time.

I strolled down the street, then remembered where I'd parked and strolled back up the street in the other direction, and finally saw my TARDIS sitting where I'd left it by the bus stop. As always, no-one paid it any attention. But it was home.

As I put the key in the lock, I wondered for a second – just the tiniest, teeniest, fractionette of a second – if I should have kept Biggles. What would it be like, having a cat in the TARDIS? Not a robot cat, not a psychic, alien, talking cat – just a cat. A normal cat. Sitting there and purring inanely and keeping you company. A Time Lord and his pet. A constant companion across all of space and time who asks for nothing more than a bit of attention, a few square meals and somewhere warm to sleep.

But then I thought – that's what humans are for.

The Body Bank

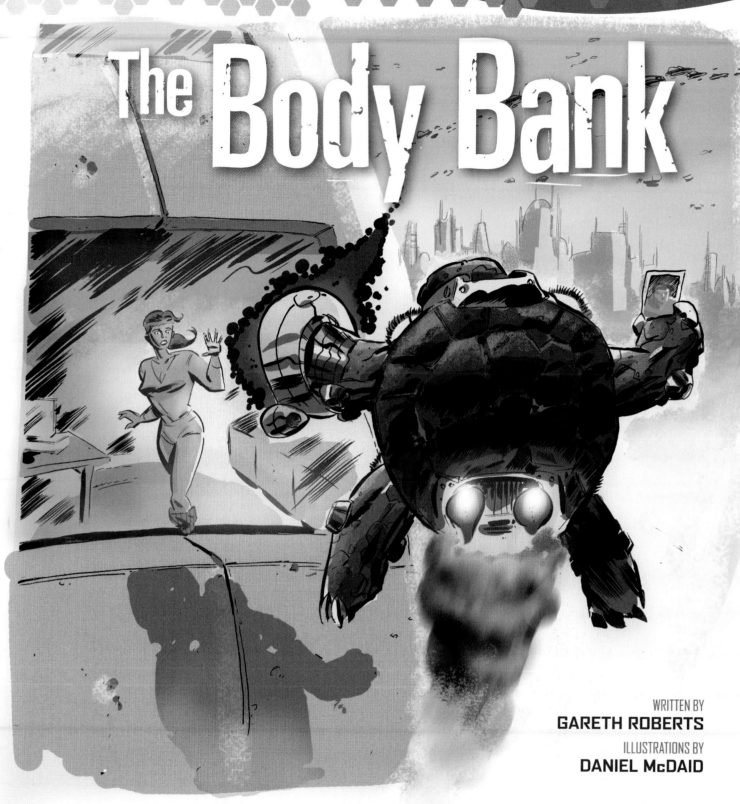

WRITTEN BY
GARETH ROBERTS

ILLUSTRATIONS BY
DANIEL McDAID

NATALIE STRETCHED HER LONG, TANNED ARMS.
She had her body back!

She stared lovingly at her reflection in the large oval mirror that covered the crack in the plasti-seal of her bedroom wall. Her eyes were blue and clear, the bags and redness gone. There were no stretch marks and veins under her arms. Her legs were toned, cellulite-free. And right next to the mirror was a wardrobe full of useless clothes, each item inside it now seven sizes too big for her.

Yes, okay, it was cheating. And yes, it had cost Natalie fifty thousand credits, three years' wages in her old job at the protein factory. But now she was vindicated. All the saving and sacrifice had been worth it.

She skipped over to the window and stared down from her apartment into the city. Hover cars and light-trams buzzed back and forth along the trafficways, ferrying the first wave of the city's workers to their jobs. Way down in the streets she could see herds of Zinords being led to market, their fur shimmering in the morning sunlight. Somebody somewhere was singing tunelessly.

Natalie smiled more fully than she ever had before. She was thin and gorgeous and, at last, life was hers for the taking.

That was the moment when an enormous tortoise dropped down from space, hovered outside the window, checked a photograph gripped in one of its claws, grunted, and fired a massive gigga-kill laser right at her.

WAY, WAY DOWN IN THE STREETS, THE HERD OF A
hundred or so Zinords Natalie had spotted were shuffling non-
committally to market under the watchful gaze of their herders,
two old hands from a farm on the eastern fringes of the city. The
older of the old hands knew something was wrong when every one
of the Zinords' ears flicked back at the same moment, and every
pair of Zinord eyes flashed with fear.

'Something's spooked 'em,' he said.

A second later a terrible wheezing, groaning sound, ancient
engines straining, split the air. Right in the middle of the herd a
lamp started to flash illogically in mid air and a strange blue shape
began to appear, fading up from transparency.

The herd bellowed, roared, and ran, kicking up clouds of dust.

The herders tore after them, stopping only to look back and
curse the idiot who had teleported a weird old wooden box right
along a prohibited cattle route.

Martha stepped from the TARDIS and coughed, fanning the
thick yellow dust away from her face. The din of the departing
stampede echoed round the tall buildings on either side. 'I think
we surprised somebody,' she spluttered. Her shoe squelched in
something soft and unpleasant on the road. 'Oh yeah. We definitely
surprised somebody.'

The Doctor emerged, taking in the situation with a glance.
'Ah. The TARDIS gets some people that way.' He pointed ahead
to a particularly large building, around which hover cars were
swarming. 'There it is! The Fraxinos Museum. In there, the biggest
collection of ancient Earth artefacts since the time of dawn. And
a pretty good café.' He started to stride purposefully off down the
road in the direction of the museum.

Martha finished scraping her shoe clean on the kerb and hurried
after him. 'Time of dawn? You mean, since "the dawn of time"'.

'No, I mean since the time of dawn,' said the Doctor. 'Space
Queen Dawn. She had a massive haul of stuff back in about, oh,
the year 300,000.'

'It's amazing,' said Martha, looking up at the glittering spires
and sky traffic. 'This is about the same time as New Earth,
yeah?' She thought back to their adventure in the
gridlocked city of New New York; the architecture
of the skyscraping buildings was similar, though
thankfully the traffic was flowing freely here.

'Couple of hundred thousand years
before,' the Doctor confirmed. He pointed.
'New Earth's about a hundred billion
parsecs that way, probably just being
colonised. Fraxinos has been settled for
thousands of years, got its own culture
and history. We're in the golden age
of Fraxinos. Never feels golden when
you're in the middle of one, you only
appreciate it when it's gone.'

Martha turned, looking right
round the city. She couldn't see any
signs of decay or poverty. 'Easy life.'

The Doctor scratched his head.
'Life's never that easy, there's always
something going pear-shaped for
somebody.'

At that moment a young woman,
tall and blonde and wearing a flimsy
nightgown, tore round a corner and
smacked straight into the Doctor,
knocking him into the dust. 'There's
this giant tortoise, it's trying to kill me!'
she shouted.

The Doctor picked himself up and
dusted himself down. He shot Martha a

'What did I tell you?' look.

'A giant tortoise?' As the question left her lips, Martha wondered why she sounded so sceptical. It was nothing stranger than many of the sights she'd seen since joining the Doctor.

'That'll be a Chelonian,' said the Doctor happily. He turned to the young woman. 'Did it have cybernetic additions?'

'Ask it,' she said, catching her breath and pointing further up the road. Martha's heart skipped a beat as a huge creature, seven foot long and four foot wide but in every other respect a tortoise, emerged from an alley, its head raised, sniffing the air. Its expression was murderous, and it carried an oddly-shaped weapon in one of its front claws.

The Doctor was beaming. 'They made it! I haven't seen a Chelonian since the 67th century, and here they are a billion years on, oh yes!'

The creature reacted to his voice, swivelling its gun to cover them. 'Step aside from that woman!' it barked, its voice gruff and so loud it echoed round the nearby buildings.

The Doctor stepped right in front of her. 'Or what?'

The Chelonian scuttled forward across the dirt track towards them with terrifying speed. Martha instinctively gripped the young woman's hand to comfort her.

'I don't want to have to kill the innocent,' the Chelonian threatened, waggling the snubby nose of its yellow gun. 'But if you protect her I have no choice!'

The Doctor seemed even more delighted. 'Aw, do you hear that?' he said. 'They've improved! Back in the old days they'd mow down anybody, then they changed their spots, and their spots stayed changed!'

'What is he talking about? Spots what?' wailed the woman, who had sunk to her knees in the dust, exhausted and terrified.

The Chelonian was now only a couple of metres from them. It stopped and raised its weapon. 'This is your final warning!'

The Doctor ferreted in his inside pocket. 'I was hoping I wouldn't have to do this. No, actually, that's a lie, I've been dying to do it.'

'Do what?' thundered the Chelonian.

'This!' said the Doctor, whipping out his sonic screwdriver and, Martha noticed, manipulating the tiny controls along its silver stem with particular care. The screwdriver emitted a slightly lower tone than its usual buzz, and the Chelonian's gun-claw shot up and froze with a grinding of concealed gears. Its huge shell sagged and its other claws retracted with a crunch.

'You've seized it up,' said Martha.

'Yes I have, all its machine bits frozen, clever me, but it's only gonna last about five minutes approx, and then he'll recalibrate,' said the Doctor, slipping the screwdriver back into his pocket. 'So no way

that's gonna work again.'

The young woman got up and stared at the powerless creature. 'We can kill it, now!'

The Doctor sighed. 'Er, no we can't. I've just rescued you, please don't make me wonder why.'

'Well, it's been trying to kill me!' she screamed.

'Yeah, and I wanna know what you've done to annoy it,' replied the Doctor.

'Who are you anyway?'

The Doctor flashed the psychic paper.

The woman read what she thought was written on it and gulped. 'You're ISDF?'

'That's us,' said the Doctor. 'Intergalactic Security/Defence Force.'

The woman pointed at them. 'Dressed like that?'

'Plain clothes. Fairly plain clothes.'

The Chelonian grunted and strained, its jaw snapping, a gurgle forming at the back of its throat.

Martha turned to the Doctor.

'You said five minutes!'

'Approx. Ish,' said the Doctor. 'You know what, I think we ought to start running.'

'But I'm exhausted!' cried the young woman.

The Chelonian growled and shuffled forward aggressively, its gun-claw clicking down several degrees.

Martha looked back down the long dirt road. 'Can't go back to the TARDIS, the road's too open, it'll cut us down.'

'This way, then,' cried the Doctor, running off round a corner. Martha grabbed the young woman's hand and tore after him. As she rounded the corner, she felt a blast of heat behind her and heard a crunch of falling masonry as the Chelonian let off a sizzling volley of shots.

'So what did you do to wind that thing up?' she asked the young woman.

'Nothing!' she cried. 'I have done absolutely nothing for the last year!'

'You must've done *something*,' shouted the Doctor as he dodged down another alleyway.

'How could I?' yelled the woman over the roar of the pursuing Chelonian's blaster fire. 'I've been in the Body Bank!'

'And suddenly everything becomes clear!' shouted the Doctor.

'Not to me it doesn't,' Martha shouted back.

'It will!' cried the Doctor. He lifted the sonic screwdriver in the air as they ran and it emitted a regular, high-pitched beep. A moment later a yellow painted sky-car with the word TAXI scrawled along one side zoomed down and hovered just ahead of them.

The driver wound down his window and looked them over, taking in the situation at a glance. 'Sorry, I'm going home,' he muttered automatically.

'Get in!' shouted the Doctor, wrenching open the door for Martha and the woman. Martha grabbed her and scrambled in.

'Oi!' shouted the taxi driver.

'Sorry, hijack!' shouted the Doctor as he vaulted in and leaned over the driver's shoulder, grabbing the wheel and aiming the sky car high, high into the upper levels and away from the rampaging Chelonian. The echoing blaster fire faded into the distance.

'That should do it,' he sighed.

'Oi!' shouted the driver.

'It can fly!' shouted the woman over the roar of the taxi's straining engine.

Martha strained to hear. 'It can what?'

'IT! CAN! FLY!' hollered the woman.

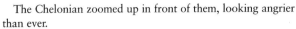

The Chelonian zoomed up in front of them, looking angrier than ever.

'Oi!' shouted the driver. Then he fainted.

'Oh great,' said the Doctor and wrenched the wheel off to one side at dizzying speed.

FIVE MINUTES OF LIGHTNING TWISTS AND TURNS later, the Doctor seemed to have shaken off the Chelonian. For Martha it was like being in the middle of a computer game as the sky-taxi zigzagged between the huge skyscrapers with bolts of blaster energy lancing just inches from them. She distracted herself by introducing herself and the Doctor and asking the woman her name.

'I'm Natalie Sharrocks,' she'd replied.

'Natalie Sharrocks?' Martha repeated, surprised.

'What's wrong with that?' Natalie asked.

Martha turned to the Doctor. 'Just sounds a bit… ordinary for the year four billion whatever.'

'What's your middle name?' the Doctor asked Natalie.

'Zentriskian, if you really must know,' she replied.

The Doctor nodded to Martha. 'There you go.'

Now, having shaken off their pursuer, they were coasting along to a very particular destination – the Body Bank Natalie had mentioned.

'What exactly is the Body Bank?' asked Martha.

Natalie frowned. 'What, you don't know? Where've you been?'

'She's from off-planet, long way away,' the Doctor called back. 'She's a yokel.'

'Thanks for that,' sighed Martha.

The Doctor pointed ahead. 'That is the Body Bank.' He was bringing the taxi to settle at a semi-circular landing bay that hugged the side of a glittering gherkin-shaped purple building.

'OK, but what is it?' demanded Martha.

'Well, I could tell you,' said the Doctor, opening the door and shooing them all out on to the platform. 'Or I could show you.' Something occurred to him and he doubled back into the front of the cab. Martha watched as he grabbed a plastic card on a string attached to the wheel and wiped the strip along the back with the sonic. 'Forgot to tip.' The card turned gold and the Doctor frowned. 'Oops, went a bit far, now he's a millionaire. Right, come on!'

He strode towards the plush reception of the Body Bank.

A FEW MINUTES – AND ANOTHER QUICK FLASH OF the psychic paper – later, the Doctor's party was being shown round the premises, on a 'routine police inspection', by an immaculately dressed and athletically good-looking young man who'd introduced himself as Colly, owner of the Body Bank. Martha thought he looked a little too perfect and symmetrical, the kind of bloke who loved the gym – and himself – more than he ever could love anybody else.

'This is the Exercise Zone,' he said, leading them into a carpeted viewing bay that looked down on to an enormous gymnasium. Down there Martha could see row after row after row of cross-trainers, treadmills and exercise bikes. Every machine was occupied by a fat person, and every one of them was throwing themselves into their routine enthusiastically.

'They're really going for it,' she said.

'That's the advantage of the process,' said Colly. 'Hand your body to us and we do all the work for you.'

Martha blinked. 'Hand my body over?'

'That's what happens here,' said the Doctor, nodding into the gym. 'You stump up the cash and rent out your body to someone else. They get it fit.'

'Rent it out?' Martha boggled. 'To who?'

'That's what I wanna know,' said the Doctor. He turned to Colly. 'Well?'

'It's all legal, officer,' he replied a little sniffily. 'Let me show you.'

He led them into the next area. Natalie groaned. 'I know all this,' she told the Doctor as they followed Colly down the hall. 'Can we deal with the tortoise thing?'

'We are dealing with it,' said the Doctor. 'Wait a bit.'

'I'm off to the cafe,' said Natalie. 'I'm exhausted!' She stalked off.

'Let her go, she was slowing us down,' said the Doctor.

Colly led them into a large, spotlessly white, room. Rows of couches like dentists' chairs were lined up along the walls. A very fat man in a tracksuit was just settling uncomfortably down on to a couch.

'Good morning Mr Catterall,' said Colly. 'Not long now.'

The fat man gave him a thumbs up. White-coated attendants hovered round him, adjusting a device that looked something like an old-fashioned hair-drier so that it pointed directly over his head.

The Doctor pointed to it and his face clouded over. 'That's a psycho-graft!'

Colly winced. 'We prefer to call it a Transfer Enabler. And it's still legal here on Fraxinos, officer.'

The attendants switched on the machine, and Martha stepped back involuntarily as a wave of green light pulsed down over the fat man's head with a violent crackling noise.

'Our client Mr Baxter's mind has now been removed,' said Colly.

'Removed to where?' asked Martha.

'The storage zone.' Colly took a small remote control from a nearby desk and pointed it at a screen that hung suspended in the air. An image appeared there, and Martha took another step back at what it showed. A giant brain hung suspended in a tank of fluid, pulsing gently. A woman stepped into shot, scattering a phial of what Martha guessed were nutrients into the tank, as if she were feeding a goldfish.

'The minds of our clients are housed in the Brain until their bodies are ready for them to pick up,' said Colly.

Martha shuddered. 'Natalie was in there? You've been in there? How could you do that to yourself?'

'The minds are unaware in the Brain,' said Colly smoothly. 'It's really very like being asleep, believe me.'

The machine emitted another shockwave, and a purple light zoomed towards the fat man's head. The attendants pulled back the hair-drier device and revealed him smiling beatifically. One of them handed him a towel and a bottle of water and he jogged happily away towards the gym.

'Right, so whose mind is in his body?' asked Martha.

'One of our trademarked Gym Minds,' replied Colly. 'A specially created consciousness, programmed for dedication to exercise.'

Martha struggled to take this in. The implications were staggering. 'You can create minds? Out of nothing?'

Colly bristled. 'All perfectly legal on this planet.'

'And illegal

everywhere else,' said the Doctor. 'An Argolin scientist made the breakthrough a few thousand years back. He called it The Soul Machine. Not to be confused with The Soul Machine disco in Harlem in the 70s, which incidentally was a lot more fun. He found a way to shape minds from the ether, carve out consciousness.'

'It's disgusting,' said Martha.

Colly smiled. 'Superstition.'

The Doctor frowned. 'Perhaps. But it upset people. Made them think about things, things nobody wants to think about. What am I, who am I, what's the mind, what's the body, etcetera. Stirred up all the belief systems, religious and secular, everybody took sides, and the balloon went up. Wars that wiped out billions.'

'That won't happen here,' said Colly, 'and this is a more enlightened age. People are always scared of new developments. The savages of the dark ages were frightened of genetic modification and nuclear power.' He glowered at Martha. 'I'd appreciate it if you didn't look at me like that.'

Anyway, we're not here for talk ethics,' said the Doctor. 'We wanna know what Natalie Sharrocks' body was doing for the last six months.'

Colly sighed. 'Like all the others, it was in the Exercise Zone. Why do you ask?'

The Doctor gestured to the remote control in Colly's hand. 'Mind if I borrow that a bit?' He took the control and adjusted the screen so that it showed a news site. At astonishing speed the Doctor scrolled through page after page until he settled on something significant. 'Here we are. A Chelonian Breeding Planet in the Perugorn Sector was destroyed in a motiveless bomb attack. Chelonian Law Enforcers are hunting a visitor to the planet, a young blonde woman. "She can't hide," says Law Chief Hezzka,

"we have her visi-print and wherever she is we'll find and execute her."' He clicked off the screen. 'Bingo. Natalie Sharrocks' body walked out of here while she was sleeping and killed thousands of unborn Chelonians.'

'No wonder they're angry,' said Martha.

'It's impossible,' said Colly. 'The Gym Minds sleep, eat and exercise, that's all they do. All they can do. I think we'd have noticed if one of them had slipped out halfway across the galaxy.'

'Why would you?' asked Martha. 'Do you keep an eye on them? If it's "impossible", why bother?'

Colly swallowed. 'This must be a mistake…'

The Doctor's tone hardened. 'Another reason why the psycho-graft got banned. There are things out there, disembodied minds, floating round, looking for somewhere to go.' He gestured to the couch where Mr Baxter had sat. 'The moment you swap the psyches of two different people they've got a split second, a window into the physical world. And not all of 'em are friendly. This one came back after it did its dirty work and passed Natalie's body back. It's the perfect crime, he got away with mass murder in broad daylight and somebody else takes the rap.'

'But Natalie is Natalie again,' said Martha. 'So the mind that took her over and bombed that planet, where did it go?'

The Doctor whistled. 'Good point, Martha Jones.' He nodded to Colly. 'When did you switch Natalie back?'

'First thing this morning.'

'And who was the next transfer?'

'You saw it happen,' said Colly. 'Mr Baxter.'

'It would be hanging round, waiting for its next chance,' said the Doctor. 'Another body to use, another crime. Now it's got one! Come on!'

He raced off towards the gym.

NATALIE TOOK ANOTHER BIG BITE OF CHOCOLATE ÉCLAIR.
The Body Bank café was designed, she suspected, to get you fat again
as soon as possible. But just this one little treat wouldn't hurt, and
she deserved it after the madness of this morning. Her mind turned
over the events, and something occurred to her. She'd been running
faster and harder than she ever had in her life, and for the first time,
nobody had burst out laughing as she puffed past. It was something
positive to take from this bizarre experience, anyway. She stared into
space for a moment and then found herself absent-mindedly dialling
up another eclair from the dispenser. One more wouldn't hurt. She'd
promised herself that she'd stick to a diet and exercise regime when
she got her body back, but all that running had taken it out of her, so
she deserved a day off.

Suddenly, just as she was finishing her second treat and
contemplating a third – perhaps a marzipan fancy, this time? – Mr
Baxter came pelting through the big swing doors into the café, gasping
for breath.

The Doctor and Martha were right behind him.

'You can't get away!' shouted the Doctor – unnecessarily, as Baxter
sagged to the floor clutching his chest.

He raised his big fat head and snarled. 'You cannot stop me!' His
voice was deeper, more sinister and much louder than it should have
been. He struggled to sit up.

The Doctor promptly sat on him. 'I just have,' he said angrily. 'Now
get out of that body, you've no place in this world!'

'Why did you do it?' demanded Martha. 'Kill all those Chelonians?'

Baxter growled and spat at her. 'Because I could! I was powerless,
drifting through the void... mind without form is nothing... then I
found a door into your world. I discovered I could do things... such
magnificent things...'

The Doctor looked deep into his eyes. 'One chance. Go, right now!'

Baxter laughed cruelly. 'Or what? What can you do to me?'

Before the Doctor could reply there was a shattering crash from the
reception area and the sound of blaster shots.

Natalie screamed.

Martha grabbed her and shoved her under a table.

Seconds later the Chelonian burst through the swing doors.

'Where is she?' demanded the Chelonian, its nostrils flaring. 'I
followed her scent-trail, she is here somewhere, answer or you all die!'

The Doctor leapt up and pointed to Baxter. 'This is who you're
after, not her!'

The Chelonian growled. 'Don't anger me!'

Baxter clambered to his feet. 'She's over... there...' He raised a
finger, but before he could point to Natalie's hiding place his face
contorted in agony and he crashed heavily back to the floor. Martha
had seen the sudden cold look that came into his eyes before, in her
years of medical training. She ran to the man's side, her fingers feeling
expertly for a pulse.

'He's dead,' Martha announced. 'The shock and stress were too
much for that body... Cardiac arrest.'

'Where is the woman?' shouted the Chelonian. It waved its gun at
the Doctor's face. 'You will answer!'

'No I will not!' the Doctor shouted back, holding up the psychic
paper once again. 'Look, come with me, I'm with the ISDF, I'll explain
everything...'

'She destroyed our breeding planet!'

'No, she didn't!' said the Doctor. 'Oh, I love reasoning with
Chelonians ... I'll just have to spell it out... Look, through there is a
psycho-graft, something used it to enter her body, it used her body to
destroy your breeding planet, then it went into that body, now that
body's dead, and it's dead too. DO. YOU. GET. IT?'

The Chelonian lowered its blaster. 'Say again?'

HALF AN HOUR LATER – AFTER THE DOCTOR HAD explained it all again three more times – the Chelonian had left the planet, soaring back up into the sky to rejoin the cruiser that awaited it in orbit around Fraxinos. At the Doctor's instruction, the mind of Mr Baxter was being retrieved from the Storage Brain, and Colly's team were using their genetic stock to grow a new body for the unfortunate man.

The Doctor and Martha were dropping Natalie back at her apartment. 'You really helped me out there, stay for some lunch,' she asked them.

'Nah, we've got a lot to do, and you've got a lot to do,' the Doctor replied.

'I've got nothing to do,' said Natalie.

'You're gonna get the psycho-graft banned on this planet,' said the Doctor.

'Why should I do that?' asked Natalie. 'Things are sorted now.'

The Doctor sighed. 'Is everyone being thick today? Shall I spell it out? Complain! And then you'll get –'

'Compensation!' cried Natalie. 'Oh yeah.'

The Doctor nodded. 'And when you tell the media your story…'

Natalie looked blank.

'They'll campaign and get the psycho-graft made illegal?' said Martha.

'That's it,' said the Doctor, clapping his hand on Martha's shoulder. 'One big case like this'll tip the public opinion. And that Chelonian'll be back in a day or two, kicking up a great big government-embarrassing diplomatic fuss if he follows my advice.'

'And I'll be famous!' said Natalie. 'But I've got nothing to wear!'

But the Doctor and Martha were already heading out.

Natalie walked back to her window and looked out at the city for the second time that day. She could see the headlines already. MY BODY WAS USED. TORTOISE FROM SPACE ATTACKED ME IN MY NIGHTIE. 'BODY BANK NEARLY KILLED ME' SAYS THIN GORGEOUS NAT.

She wondered where to begin. Probably best not to set to work in her new life on an empty stomach. It was only fair, after her ordeal, to have a little celebration treat first.

So she picked up her communicator and ordered a pizza. One wouldn't hurt.

THE END

The Box Under

WRITTEN BY **ROBERT SHEARMAN**   ILLUSTRATIONS BY **MARTIN GERAGHTY**

MRS GODWIN WAS OFF SICK, OR HAVING BABIES, or dead. No-one really seemed to know the truth, but that didn't stop the rumours flying round the classroom. Harry didn't like the replacement teacher much; she smiled, but never *properly*, never with her eyes, so it always came out a bit sarcastic. She had a fat flabby face. And she didn't like Harry's attempts at English composition.

"It's a good story, though, isn't it?" Harry interrupted her.

"Yes, it *is* a good story," said the teacher, with a politeness that suggested she had severe doubts even about that. "But if you'll let me finish. It's not the *right* sort of good story, is it? I asked you for something Christmassy. And instead you've given me something about, what? A space war between these giant squids…"

"The Xarantharax," said Harry helpfully.

"And talking cows with snakes growing out of their eyes."

"The Iska'lanz'rm."

"Oh, so that's how you pronounce it."

"The cows are really evil," said Harry. "The squids are just a bit misguided. I've got to a really good bit, I think. You'll never guess what the Xarantharax and the Iska'lanz'rm have got up their sleeves next. Not that they actually have sleeves. Do you like the drawings?" he went on, taking the school exercise book back from her, and pointing out a really good one with laser beams and explosions in it.

"Hmm," said the teacher. "Not very Christmassy, though." And that was as far as she could be drawn on the quality of his artistry. She closed her eyes and sighed. "Put me out of my misery. Tell me, at some point, that the squids and the cows start giving presents to each other. Or get involved in some sort of snowball fight."

"No," said Harry. "Why would they do that?"

Harry knew exactly what Christmas was all about, so what was the point in writing about it? His Christmas would be the same as everybody else's Christmas, he imagined. They'd put the tree up next week, there'd be a spot of carol singing maybe, and relatives he hadn't seen since last year would pop over on Boxing Day and give him presents he didn't want. (No, really. Aunt Muriel bought him, of all things, toiletries. Yes. Toiletries. She was very proud of her toiletries, and somehow contrived, it seemed to Harry, to get them into every single conversation she ever had.)

Even now, at the thought of all the festive toiletries that were no doubt being prepared for him, Harry's eyes glazed over so completely that he didn't hear what his teacher was saying. And it was only when she took back his exercise book, shut it in her wooden desk, and locked it with a key, that he snapped out of it. "What are you doing?" he said, alarmed. "That's my story!"

"I'm confiscating it," said the teacher, and there wasn't a hint of a smile this time, not even a sarcastic one. "I want the essay I asked for, and I think you'll be better off with a fresh book to write in. Those pictures you've drawn will just distract you. Too much imagination," she boomed, "is just asking for anarchy."

◆ ● ◆ ● ◆

HARRY WARE WAS A BOY BLESSED WITH A FERTILE imagination. But, it had to be said, it didn't feel like a blessing most of the time. Life had this sneaking habit of being considerably less dramatic than he expected. When his Dad would phone to say he'd be late home from the office, Harry would wonder whether it was because he was really a secret agent spying for the Government and had been sent on a secret mission. Or that perhaps he'd been abducted by aliens – again! – and was unavoidably detained on one of the moons of Neptune. But the reasons his Dad was late were always so mundane – the office photocopier had jammed, or there'd been a traffic jam, or his secretary had gone down with a mild case of mumps. Anything but the excuse that would have thrilled Harry and put a spring into his step. Every night he'd

the Tree

dream that he was special, *unique*; that his bedroom wasn't really a bedroom at all, that behind the wardrobe was a portal to another universe; that his little sister wasn't really a human at all, but some sort of experimental rodent walking on its hind legs; that, to be blunt, Harry wasn't plain old Harry. And the daily disappointment he'd feel, waking up and finding out he was just a Harry after all, was sometimes more than he could bear.

And it was for this reason, on this particular Christmas morning, that he decided to get up before his parents and get a sneak preview of the presents waiting for him under the tree. He had several friends who did the same thing – they'd put the alarm clock under the pillow to muffle the sound, then downstairs they'd creep, have a peek beneath the wrapping, then do up the presents again so no-one would be any the wiser. But whereas they couldn't resist finding out what toys they'd been given, all Harry wanted was ample warning. For weeks now the pile of

parcels had been growing, all in brightly coloured shiny paper, tantalising him with what wonders they could be concealing – something alien maybe, extraterrestrial treasure! Better that he feel the disappointment now so that he could keep it from his face later; he didn't want to hurt his family's feelings.

The first surprise was that there was a package there that hadn't been there the night before. He turned the tree lights on so that he could get a better look. Eight foot tall, oblong, an enormous box – it dominated the room, dwarfed the other presents around it. Harry wondered briefly how on earth they had got it through the door in the first place. It couldn't be for him, though, surely? But it was. He read the tag, hanging from a fold of the festive wrapping paper – a jolly Santa Claus having a snowball fight with a whole army of reindeer. "To Harry," it said. And nothing else, no clue who it might be from. He reached out and touched it, and beneath the paper it was as if he could feel it *hum*.

The second surprise was that he was, in fact, surprised. It had been years since he'd had a present that had done that. It almost wouldn't matter now what it actually was, it had done its job. But that didn't mean he wasn't going to peel off the paper anyway and look. And he did.

Underneath there was a uniform blue, and at first it looked a bit drab in contrast to the gaudy wrapping paper. But the more that Harry looked at it – and the more he uncovered, because he couldn't help it, he was stripping away the paper now, he *had* to see what this box was – Harry could see that there was something odd about the blue. As if it wasn't really a blue at all. As if it was some other colour, something Harry couldn't even imagine, *pretending* to be a blue; this strange alien colour had sat down, done its homework on Blueness and All Things Relating To Blue, and this was what it had come up with. It was a *disguise*. Then lettering. "POLICE PUBLIC CALL BOX." Harry's brain flipped at that, began to work out what it could possibly mean, then decided to put it to one side for further flipping later. Because before too long Harry had uncovered something that was much more flipworthy – a large door, set inside one of the blue-but-not-blue slats.

Harry pushed against it tentatively, as if afraid it might open. It didn't. So he pushed against it more forcefully, now *wanting* it to open. It still didn't. And he saw there was a lock, so he'd need a key. Where was he going to get the key from?

And then he remembered what happened last Saturday at the department store...

HARRY HAD HAD NO GREAT DESIRE TO VISIT THE grotto. He was too old now, surely? And the weekend before

Christmas the queue to see Santa was so long, it stretched all the way round and round Soft Furnishings and ended up in the lingerie department. But when Mum had suggested they should give it a miss this year his sister had begun to cry, and stamped her foot, and she was still at an age when foot stamping had some sway in an argument. So they all stood in line for over an hour, Harry bored, Mum bored, the sister jumping up and down with excitement and singing the first line of Rudolph the Red-Nosed Reindeer over and over again, before at last they reached the entrance to the little cave. The sister went in, and emerged a few minutes later, a grin all over her face, and carrying a little gift and a balloon.

"Your go, Harry," his mum had said, and Harry had shrugged. And this was the funny thing. Harry could have sworn he'd said, "That's okay, Mum," and they'd all gone home. But now here was a different memory altogether. How very odd.

"Your go, Harry," Mum said. "Okay, Mum, I won't be long," Harry replied, and in he went.

Santa Claus sat in a tall chair, surrounded by tinsel and lights and baubles and stuff. He waved at Harry as he came in. They clearly hadn't made much effort finding a good one this year. He was too thin for a start. He was all but drowning in his big red coat. "Hello," Santa said brightly, "And ho ho ho. Yeah. You're Harry, right? I've been waiting for you for *ages*."

His sister must have given Santa Harry's name. "Your beard's falling off," said Harry. He wasn't criticising. Well, not very much. He just wanted to be helpful.

"What?" said Santa. "That shouldn't happen!" He patted at his face desperately. "It should be fused to my face, y'see, using molecular cohesion technology derived from the rings of

Saturn. Impregnable, in theory. But if Saturn's orbit is eccentric, and let's face it, it's been barking mad recently... Hmm." He smiled at Harry a little sheepishly. "Should have used sellotape, I suppose."

"I think you should know I don't believe in you," said Harry. "Sorry."

Santa blinked. "Oh," he said. "Right," he added. And then, "But I'm here, aren't I?" Harry agreed this was the case. "You're a bit young to go doubting all the magic of the world, aren't you? I was at least two hundred years old before I doubted the existence of Father Christmas. And you know what?" And Santa spoke more quietly, and Harry had to bend in closer to listen, in spite of himself. "*I was wrong.*"

"If you say so," said Harry.

"Got to keep believing in things, Harry," said Santa, and although he was smiling, there was a steel to his voice. "Cos you've just *got* to."

"Okay," said Harry.

Santa relaxed in his seat. "Round about now I'd do the 'what do you want for Christmas' bit. You know the sort of thing."

Harry nodded. For a moment he thought he might actually try to tell Santa what he really hoped for – he knew that it was too new and too odd and too wonderful to be expressed in mere words, he wouldn't know where to start. But with this Santa he thought he might actually try. Instead he sighed, and tried to remember what all the boys in class went on about, that'd be safer. He said mechanically, "I'd like an X-box, please."

"Nah," said Santa, and his arms flapped comically in the enormous sleeves as he reached into his sack. "I know what you're after. And here it is." He held it out to him. "It's a key," he said, and dropped it into Harry's palm.

Harry looked at it blankly. Opened his mouth to say something. Didn't.

"Useful things, keys," Santa went on, barely pausing for breath. "Exciting too! Wish I'd had a key at your age, you'll be the envy of all your friends. Although, on second thoughts, I wouldn't make a big deal about it, I wouldn't tell them if I were you. Actually, on third thoughts, don't tell anybody, keep it to yourself. Look after the key, Harry," he said urgently, "remember the key."

Harry found his voice at last. "What do I do with it?"

"Oh, use your imagination," said Santa. And Harry realised it wasn't a rebuke, it was a genuine piece of advice. Use his imagination. Remember the key.

But he'd forgotten it, hadn't he? Now, on Christmas morning, with the lock staring him in the face, at last Harry remembered. Where was it? The jacket he'd worn last weekend. Which one was it? He found it hanging by the front door, rummaged through the pockets. And there, at the bottom of everything, sweet wrappers, bus tickets, hardened bits of chewing gum, was the present he'd been given by the thin Santa Claus with the droopy beard. It hummed in his hand insistently, just like the blue box. It was so loud he was worried it might wake his parents up, and he wondered why he'd never heard it before.

It was obvious it was the right key – it almost leaped into the lock, as if running for home. It turned easily, and Harry prepared to squeeze into the tiny cupboard space inside.

Of course, it wasn't a cupboard. And it wasn't tiny. And Harry was surprised for the third time that day.

The previous summer Harry's mum had had a new kitchen fitted. She'd clearly been very proud of it, and had told all of her friends how the design was 'very organic'. She used the word 'organic' rather a lot; all Harry saw was that the handles on the kitchen drawers were a little more curvy. Standing inside

the blue box, and goggling at its sheer *size*, he at last understood what 'organic' meant, and it was everything his mum's kitchen wasn't. It was as if everything around him had grown – the gantries, the supports, and the peculiar mushroom-shaped dais in the middle of the room. Harry had the sudden sensation he was standing inside a living being, and as soon as he thought it he knew that was it, he was absolutely right. He supposed he should be frightened by the idea of that, but in a way he had never felt more safe or more at home.

He took a closer look at the console. Switches and levers and buttons were fighting for space on it; some as futuristic as

Harry's wildest space story imaginings, others the sort of things that'd look old-fashioned in Grandad's garage. He was itching to play with them, could almost feel them urging him to give them a prod. "It's a spaceship," Harry said out loud, "these are the controls for a *spaceship*." Press the right button, he decided, and he could go anywhere in the universe. No, more than that, why not? – it could go anywhere in time as well. It was up to him to set limits on what this machine was capable of, and he decided there weren't going to be *any* limits, not any more. Use your imagination, Santa had said. And so he was going to do just that.

But which buttons to press? Which levers to throw? He stood there in an agony of indecision. And then he remembered what had happened last Tuesday at the chemist's...

"HERE," DAD HAD SAID, "HERE'S A FIVER TO GO WITH your pocket money. Now go and buy your Mum something that'll make her happy." And he'd taken Harry into the town centre, left him to look around the shops. But Harry had no idea what would make Mum happy – he'd lived with her every day for nearly thirteen years and he'd never even begun to work that one out. Perfume, he thought. She'd like perfume, probably. Well, it'd worked last year. And the year before.

There was a crowd of people bustling around the perfume counter buying Christmas gifts. Only one shop assistant wasn't being harassed on all sides, standing in the middle of them all, blissfully relaxed. Harry wondered for a second why everyone was ignoring her, and then took advantage of the fact and went straight for her. "Hello," he said. "What's the best perfume you can get with eight pounds fifty?"

The girl was tall, dark-skinned and very beautiful. "Don't know," she said cheerfully, "but let's take a look, I like a challenge! How about this?" She picked a bottle off the shelf, looked at it curiously. "Aroma, it's called. Oh, very original!"

"Sounds a bit..." and Harry screwed up his nose.

The girl screwed up her nose too. "Yeah, it does a bit. Still, let's give it a go!" And before he could stop her, she'd taken hold of his hand, and sprayed a bit on to Harry's wrist. Great, he thought, I'm going to stink for ages. They both sniffed at the wet patch, one after the other, both pulled faces.

"That's pretty foul, isn't it?" said the shop assistant.

"Yeah," said Harry.

"Tell you what," said the assistant. "Don't bother with perfume. How about a set of flight instructions instead? Yeah," she went on, as if enthused by this new idea, "that'll be good. Here you are." She produced, as if from nowhere, a set of blueprints and handed them to Harry.

"I don't know," said Harry dubiously. "You think my Mum will like it?"

"God, no!" said the girl, and laughed. "This is for you, Harry. It's for you." A customer tapped her on the shoulder. "Just a moment, sir," she said, "I'm serving this gentleman first."

Harry looked at the sheet of paper, on which seemed to be nothing more instructive than a series of squiggles in marker pen. He looked up at the girl, who smiled so encouragingly at him that he thought it'd be rude not to smile back. "That's it," she said. "You understand now, don't you? The key's all very well, but it's not much good getting into a place if you don't know what to do once you're inside." His smile evidently wobbled, because she frowned. "You remember the key, don't you? Oh, come on, Harry. Remember the key."

"Yes," said Harry vaguely. "There was a key..."

The customer harrumphed for attention again. "Just a *minute*, sir," said the shop assistant, and turned to look at him. "Oh," she said. The customer harrumphed again, but it wasn't a human harrumph – and this made perfect sense when you realised he wasn't human. He had instead the face of a squid, and tentacles were issuing from his cheeks, lashing towards the girl.

Harry looked around wildly, but no-one else seemed to notice – they were too busy fighting for last-minute savings on toiletries. Without even stopping to think, he grabbed hold of the Aroma bottle, and giving a victory cry he hoped would sound blood-curdling and impressive but he suspected sounded just a little bit embarrassing, he sprayed the perfume

straight into the squid's face.

The effect was immediate. The tentacles let go of the assistant, the harrumphing turned to a squealing, and the monster ran away into the crowd. "Are you all right?" asked Harry. And then, with no little pride, "I remember the key!"

The girl looked none the worse for wear. "That's good, Harry," she said, getting her breath back. "The key *and* the instructions. Two things to remember. It's very important you remember."

Harry nodded, stuffed the paper into the satchel. Already the attack of the monster seemed a distant memory, nothing to get too excited about. There were other things he needed to ask. "And what about a present for my Mum?"

"Oh," said the assistant confidentially, "if you want my advice, don't bother with cheap perfume. She'll wear it once to be polite, then pour it down the sink. Get her a nice box of chocs instead. Everyone likes chocs."

SO HARRY RETRIEVED THE INSTRUCTIONS FROM HIS satchel. What had first appeared to be no more than random squiggles now made perfect sense. He stabbed at buttons and pulled at levers as suggested ("Give this one a bit of welly," the note said helpfully, "it sometimes gets a bit stuck"). And then, as if the beast he'd been standing in all this time had just been dozing, the living blue box *woke up*, it yawned and stretched itself awake. And suddenly there was a noise of – what, engines? Or something like coughing? – and they were on their way,

Harry didn't know where, and he couldn't help but laugh with the excitement of it all. And then the coughing stopped, the doors were flung open – and outside he could see… nothing. Absolutely nothing. He went to the doors and looked out. "Oh," he said. As exclamations went it was hardly equal to the occasion, but it was the best he could come up with in the shock of the moment.

It wasn't nothing, not at all; it was *space*. Beneath his feet planets spun and stars dazzled – and, even as he marvelled at them, they were obscured as spaceships flew into view, big and bold and bulky, with cannons and guns and *everything*. The ships that looked a bit like flying saucers fired on the ships that looked a bit like tanks, and the laser beams were purple and green and silverish. Harry supposed he ought to have been frightened, standing this close to an intergalactic war, but if anything it felt like home, that what he'd been dreaming of in his head for so long was there to see at last. As he watched one of the spaceships explode into a burst of flame, the view beneath him slowed down, then froze. And Harry realised why it all seemed so familiar. "This is my story," he said out loud. "This is *my* picture."

The blue box gave a grunt that might have been congratulatory, the doors slammed, the floor shuddered, and Harry was travelling again.

Once again the doors opened, and Harry prepared himself for… what? An alien planet? Pink skies and twin suns? What he saw instead was a row of lockers. And not alien lockers either, these were your common or garden lockers. He couldn't help but

opened the door to the classroom and went in.

He didn't have a clue what was going on, but Harry knew it had to be *something* to do with that story he'd written. He tried to get it from the teacher's desk, but it was locked. He wondered whether the key Santa had given him might open it – but it was no use, it was great for getting him into magical boxes that took him through space and time, but absolutely rubbish with wooden drawers. "You've worked it out, haven't you?" said his teacher, and Harry looked up, startled.

"I'm sorry, Miss…" and Harry tried to finish her name – and then realised that he'd never known it, she'd never given it to them.

"You can't be allowed to finish it," said the teacher. And she reached up to her flabby face, picked hold of a layer of fat hanging from the chin, and with a sucking sound that quite turned Harry's stomach pulled *upwards*. She threw the mask to one side. Her cow face glared at Harry balefully, the eyes growing into snakes, unwinding and lashing at him with a hiss.

"You're a Iska'lanz'rm," said Harry.

"We never knew how to pronounce it," rumbled what had been his teacher. "None of us could work it out, what with all the apostrophes. It's good that you've told me how to say my name before I kill you. You can't be allowed to finish it, you see." The monster advanced towards him, snake eyes ever extending, reaching for his throat. "You can't finish the *picture*."

And then it struck Harry that although he should now be horribly frightened, he wasn't. He was just angry. This was something he'd created, he'd come up with the apostrophes all by himself, it was hard to think of a good name and it had taken him *ages*. No-one appreciated his stories, his parents were too busy to read them, the teachers confiscated them – and when at last someone *did* take them seriously, they grew snake eyes and tried to throttle him. Well, he wasn't going to stand for it. With a strength he didn't know he had, he pushed the big desk over. It crashed to the floor, and the cow jumped back so it wouldn't hurt its hooves. Then with a battle cry Harry heaved at the desk with all his might – it scooped up the Iska'lanz'rm, knocked it off its feet, and sent it sprawling back out of the classroom. Harry slammed the door, barricaded it with the desk, and realised, gasping, panting for breath, that he could have played for the hockey team after all.

The monster gave an insane bellow and battered against the glass. Harry saw that in the crash the desk drawer had been smashed open. He grabbed hold of the exercise book, flicked to the page where he'd drawn the space battle he'd witnessed. He wouldn't be allowed to finish it? Well, it was *his* story, and he'd do what he liked! He stared at the picture, and it was just as he remembered – the laser beams, the spaceships, the ginormous explosions.

And Harry went cold… It *was* finished, wasn't it? It was exactly as he'd seen it from the blue box. What did the monster mean? There was nothing to add!

The bellowing grew louder, the smashing against the door

feel a little disappointed; he stepped out of the box, and realised that he was in the corridor leading down to his classroom. The school should have been shut up for the Christmas holidays, surely – but as he peered through the glass of the classroom door, he saw something which shocked him even more than the solar system ablaze. "Oh," he whispered, no longer even bothering to try at an appropriate exclamation. This was too big a shock to worry about things like that.

"It's a good story, though, isn't it?" said a little boy to a teacher, and the little boy was *him*. He saw the teacher with the cold eyes and the sarcastic non-smile take his story, shut it away in her desk. Then both of them made to leave the room. Quick as a flash, Harry made himself look as inconspicuous as possible, and pointedly studied the notice board as if he were particularly fascinated by the activities of the Year Eight girls' hockey team. His heart steadied and he allowed himself a sigh of relief when both teacher and the other him passed by without giving him a second look. And, once he was sure the coast was clear, he more powerful. There were other cows out there now, all trying to get in. And they'd been joined by the giant squids. "You mustn't finish the picture!" bellowed the Iska'lanz'rm. "You *shan't* finish the picture!" agreed the Xarantharax, their voices shrill and hissing.

Harry stared back at the picture. And realised what was missing from it. He searched the drawer for a blue crayon.

A hole was punched in the door. An Iska'lanz'rm got a hoof through. A Xarantharax joined it with something like a sucker.

No blue crayon to be seen! Harry checked again, desperately. There was a green and a pink and a sort of mauve and a...

"Now we have you!" cried the cow in triumph, as the glass shattered entirely.

"It'll have to do," said Harry, and picked up the first crayon he could. And in the upper right hand corner of his picture drew a little box, hovering over the battle...

"AT LAST!" SAID SANTA. "I KNEW YOU'D GET THERE in the end!" He charged through the door, elbowing cows and squid aside, and the shop assistant from Boots followed on his heels. "Well done, Harry, that is your name isn't it, yes, good. Here, take this."

"What is it?"

"It's a sonic atomiser," said Santa. He was now dressed in a blue pin-striped suit which fitted him better than the Father Christmas garb – when he waved his arms excitedly, as he did now, the sleeves didn't flap about as comically. "Ideal for spraying out vast quantities of cheap scent in concentrated form." He and the shop assistant were spraying to their heart's content at each rampaging monster that got too close – Harry swiftly followed their example. A Xarantharax reached out to grab him; he gave it a quick blast, and it dissolved into thin air with a despondent snarl. "Good idea about the perfume, by the way, love it," said Santa. "Never underestimate toiletries. Rubbish as Christmas presents, but good for defeating the odd alien monster."

The armies were thinning out by now, as the three heroes stood in the classroom, firing out 'Aroma – For Women' in all directions. Harry wished he'd thought up a better weapon – effective it may have been, but it didn't half make a stink. It was all so exciting it took him a good minute or so to think to ask what on earth was going on.

"It's like this," said Santa. "There are millions and millions of stories out there. *Trillions.* But sometimes the storyteller is *so* good, his imagination is *so* powerful, that it leaves an imprint on the universe. The stories can't help but come true."

"Like mine?" said Harry, and felt incredibly pleased.

"You've got to keep writing," said Santa, "you've got a brilliant gift. But, you know, in this case, you hadn't written Martha and I in to sort the whole thing out. We weren't able to join your story until you had."

"Right," said Harry. And thought about this. And then said, "But you *did* take part. You were in Santa's grotto. You were in Boots."

"That's what I said to him," said the shop assistant.

"Well, not *really*," said Santa. "Well, not as ourselves. Well, just to give you a helpful nudge in the right direction. Well," he said, "I cheated, just a little bit."

Harry fired at the last Iska'lanz'rm – he thought this one had been his teacher. "What did we do?" he asked. "Did we kill them?"

"That's up to you," said Santa.

Harry thought for a bit. "I think the perfume just takes them back to their own planet," he said. "They're alive, but can't bother us again."

Santa nodded approvingly. "Nice one," said the shop assistant.

They walked back into the corridor. Santa stared at his box. "What have you done?" he said at last.

"I couldn't find a blue crayon," said Harry.

"But it's orange! Not just orange, it's *bright* orange, that's not even a subdued orange, that's a right-in-your-face orange, I can't

go around… oh, I don't know though," he said, and grinned. "Mustn't be afraid of change, I've always liked oranges. What do you think, Martha?"

Martha smirked, wrinkled up her nose. "Right," said Santa. "Right." He dug into his pockets, produced a whole box of Crayola. "If it's no bother," he said to Harry, "would you mind changing it back…?"

It didn't take long for Harry to correct the picture, and put the finishing touches to his tale of alien cows and squids and boxes bigger inside than out. Santa read it when he was done.

"It's a good story, though, isn't it?" asked Harry.

Santa considered. "The ending was all right," he said. "At least you didn't do that he-woke-up-and-it-was-all-a-dream thing. That's really annoying. Well, now that you've finished the story, Martha and I are free to leave. Expect you'll wake up in bed, find it was all a dream." He smiled and turned to go.

"That's not fair," said Harry. "Can't I at least keep the key? It was supposed to be a present, wasn't it?"

"I think he deserves that much," said Martha.

Santa thought about this. "Well, okay," he said. "The key's yours. But only as long as you *remember* it. You understand, Harry? Got to keep your imagination alive if you want to remember the key."

The next thing Harry knew was his alarm clock ringing under his pillow. He thought about going downstairs to check the presents as he'd planned – but he knew now there'd be no blue box there, and couldn't quite see the point. He sighed, reached his hand under the pillow to turn off the insistent beeps. And there was a clunk of

metal as he brushed against the snooze button.

He brought out his hand. It was curled tight into a fist. It didn't want to open up, it was so keen not to let go of whatever it was hiding, and he had to prise the fingers apart manually. The key inside didn't look all that impressive, really. A bit rusted, somewhat worn around the edges through overuse. And it certainly didn't hum. It could have been the key to any old rubbish, there was nothing to say it was special, *unique*.

But he knew it was. That's really all that mattered. And he also knew that, although it wasn't obvious at first glance, he was too.

HARRY KEPT THE KEY IN HIS POCKET AS HE UNWRAPPED all his presents that day. And whenever there was a threat of disappointment, he'd finger its teeth and smile. So he was able to smile as he opened up the latest set of toiletries from Auntie Muriel.

And a few days after the holiday were over, and all the turkey had been eaten, and all the decorations were taken down, Harry turned back to his exercise book. He tried to write about the usual Christmas stuff, really he did. But before too long the story had changed completely, and it told of boxes bigger inside than out, of travel through time and space. And of a man who was a bit like Santa Claus, but something more magical besides. "The Doctor," said Harry, "that'd be a good name for him." So that's what he called him.

THE END

'DO NOT DISTURB'.

That's what the sign on the door of room 413 said. But Mr and Mrs Parker had already checked out. Lyn had seen them herself, manhandling their luggage down the corridor and into the lift. She had been cleaning up room 416 at the time, coming out with a bundle of linen for the trolley. She had even nodded hello and waved them goodbye.

Must be a mistake. Lyn sighed and yawned. She was still nowhere near the end of her shift. Whoever said being a chamber maid was an easy way to earn some cash during the summer holidays? It was back-breaking work. Cleaning up other people's mess. Up and down the seven floors of the luxurious Hotel Splendide on the outskirts of Bramlington-on-Sea.

It didn't seem so luxurious now, after a month. She fetched out the right key and let herself into room 413. Ignoring the DO NOT DISTURB sign.

'Hello..?' she said nervously as she stepped into the room. Curtains drawn. Lights out. Curious smell. Something rotting. Something chemical.

'Is there someone in here?' Lyn advanced into the room. She felt for the light switch.

And touched something soft and fleshy instead. An arm. Somebody was standing there.

Cold and sticky to the touch. Before she even knew what was happening, the arm twisted and grabbed her wrist.

And Lyn screamed and screamed and found she couldn't stop.

● ● ⬡ ●

IN THE GLITZY CHROME-AND-VELVET RECEPTION area downstairs in the Hotel Splendide, the Doctor and Martha were having morning coffee and trying to look like casual visitors. Martha glanced across the table at the Doctor and almost laughed. He couldn't look casual and relaxed if he tried. His bright eyes were flicking about all over the place, examining the hotel guests and staff as they moved through the lobby about their business.

'It seems normal enough to me,' Martha said, blowing on her Moccachino.

'But it's not,' the Doctor murmured, doing that quizzical thing with his eyebrows. 'The TARDIS was picking up some very funny readings.' He was alert with his jaggedly-cut hair standing on end.

Zombie Motel

WRITTEN BY
PAUL MAGRS

ILLUSTRATIONS BY
BEN WILLSHER

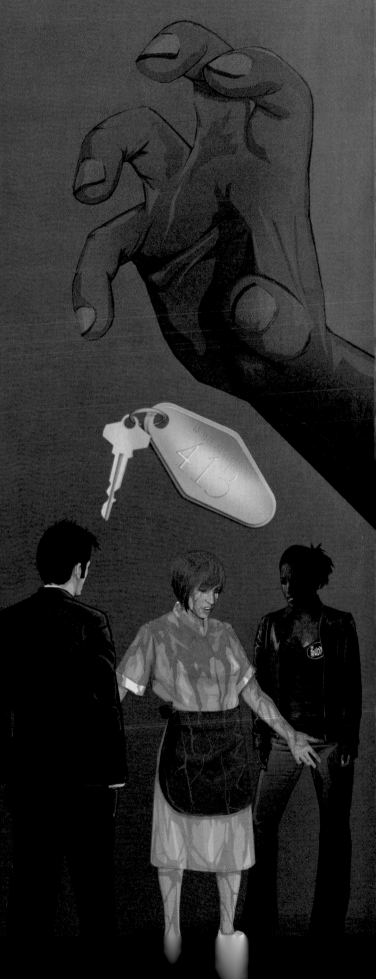

'The thing is, this place rings a bell. Something... spooky, I think. Why don't I keep a diary? Diaries are good! I'd know where I was if I kept a proper diary.'

Martha couldn't imagine the Doctor sitting still long enough to write a diary. He glugged back his scalding espresso.

'It's only been open a few weeks,' she said. 'Were you here in the future, maybe?'

'Hmmm... a hotel in Bramlington-on-Sea,' he mused. 'It's still ringing a great big, bonging, spooky old bell tolling out death and disaster!'

As if on cue, the lift doors gave a sudden PING! and swooshed open. An ear-splitting shriek rang across the lounge area.

Everyone whirled about to see who was making the noise. The Doctor leapt out of his seat and ran to the figure that emerged, shambling, whimpering, from the elevator.

Lyn was covered in evil-smelling green gunk. Everyone's eyes were on the demented chamber maid as she screeched at them all:

'It's in Room 413! It grabbed me and... said that we're all going to die! We're all going to be killed!'

The Doctor tried to placate her: 'It's all right now...'

'Then... it exploded... into pieces... into all this slime...!'

'SO WHAT HAVE WE GOT?' THE DOCTOR PULLED AT his hair distractedly and paced around Room 413. 'Exploding zombies in a luxury hotel. Telling people they'll be killed. Poisonous slime. Is that everything?'

Martha shrugged. 'Poor old Lyn wasn't in much of a state to tell us any more than that.'

Lyn was in hospital, under heavy sedation. Strapped to a stretcher, she had managed to gibber that the 'person' who had grabbed her in Room 413 had once been a tall, smartly dressed man. She had seen as much by the light of the open doorway. But she had also seen that his flesh was suppurating and green. It was this that had sent the chamber maid into hysterics.

'It does smell odd,' Martha frowned. 'Sort of... fusty and mouldy. But with a weird chemical smell, too.'

'I thought that,' the Doctor said. Thanks to the ever-useful Psychic Paper, the worried management of the Hotel Splendide were keen to let him examine the apparently haunted room. He quickly took samples of the green gunk of the zombie's footprints and the splashes on the walls that were all that was left of the awful apparition.

A knock at the door. The manager, Mr Preston in his shiny shoes and brylcreemed hair, was looking nervous as the Doctor poked his head around the door. 'Yep?'

'A Mrs Wiggins, an elderly regular user of our leisure facilities...'

'What about her?' frowned the Doctor.

'She's had an episode in the sauna and jacuzzi complex, I'm afraid.'

The Doctor blinked. 'An episode?'

'Another encounter, Doctor,' said Mr Preston. He was keeping his voice down, as other guests passed by on their way to the lifts. 'With one of these green and slimy... things...'

Martha's head appeared round the door next to the Doctor's. 'Did it say anything to her?'

IT TURNED OUT THAT THE CREATURE HAD, IN FACT, addressed Mrs Wiggins in the sauna. Clutching her towel in terror, the old woman had sat there while the zombie intoned: 'Get out of the Hotel Splendide! Let our souls rest in peace! Abandon this luxury hotel or we will destroy you all!'

Now the old woman was shaking and rocking on a chair in Mr Preston's office. The Doctor crouched down and stared into her transfixed eyes, as if he could see the zombie still reflected there.

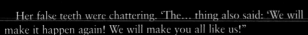

Her false teeth were chattering. 'The… thing also said: 'We will make it happen again! We will make you all like us!''

'Now, what on earth can that mean?' the hotel manager asked irritably, leading his investigators out of the office. 'Has she gone crazy?'

The Doctor murmured: 'I think it was a genuine message… from the past.' He glared at Mr Preston. 'There have been other 'episodes', haven't there?'

'Yes,' sighed the manager, hanging his head. 'Ever since we opened, a month ago. Ghostly guests… phantom hotel staff. All dripping slime and accosting people. We've tried to shush them up. But it's getting harder… The visitations are becoming weirder… more violent…' Now Mr Preston passed a hand over his tired face. 'This place is meant to be the crowning glory of the Splendide chain of leisure complexes!'

'Well,' said the Doctor off-handedly. 'I reckon you can forget that. Green dripping zombies jumping out on guests? Not a great selling point for a weekend break.'

The manager whimpered and Martha led him off to make sure he called an ambulance for the shaken old woman. 'Tactful…' she smiled at the Doctor, but saw that he wasn't even listening.

The Doctor, deep in thought, slipped off to the staff car park, where the TARDIS was waiting. He wanted to run a few tests on his samples of zombie slime…

MARTHA WATCHED AS THE SECOND AMBULANCE OF the day was loaded with a terrified occupant.

What were these things? Why were they so insistent on making themselves apparent and plaguing the inhabitants of the Hotel Splendide? Then she saw that the elderly receptionist at the main desk was calling her over. The woman was extremely skinny and rather elegant, with large earrings and her hair piled up. 'I'm Margery Darcy,' she said to Martha, sotto voce. 'And I hear that you are looking into our little mystery here at the Splendide.'

Martha nodded. 'Do you know anything?'

'Yes…,' the husky-voiced woman tapped her beaky nose. 'I… I rather think I do. I think I've seen something like this before…'

Martha was agog. 'When? Where was this?'

The glamorous old woman said: 'Right here. Before you were even born, probably. In the Motel that used to be here.' Suddenly a worried look flitted across Margery's face. 'I can trust you, can't I?'

Martha nodded. 'Of course. We're here to help.'

Margery nodded. 'The Ringroad Motel burned down. In 1979 on Hallowe'en. There was a cocktail party here at the time. Local dignitaries and valued guests. Almost everyone perished in the ghastly inferno. Almost everyone.'

Martha stared

at her. 'You were there?'

Margery nodded. 'In 1979 I was a young receptionist that the manageress, Mrs Hamilton, was training up. And I was the only survivor of that terrible Hallowe'en. And I believe I know what went on.'

Martha frowned. 'You think it's linked? With what's happening now?'

'I recognise the signs. We're being haunted by the ghosts of 1979.' Her face had turned ghastly and pale. 'Something terrible was done to them, that night back then. I knew they should never have built this hotel in the same spot! They are determined to make us pay…'

'I need to tell the Doctor this,' Martha said urgently. 'Will you talk to him?'

Margery looked lost. 'I can't leave reception. And…' Her eyes widened. 'I've never told anyone the truth of what happened that night. My memories are confusing…' Then she made up her mind. 'But I must go and ask Anne-Marie to take care of the reception desk first.'

Martha nodded impatiently and watched the old woman scurry out.

MARGERY DARCY WAS SURPRISED NOT TO FIND Anne-Marie at the formica table in the staff room.

Instead, the long-dead Irene Hamilton was sitting there. The manageress's hair was freshly set in a magenta perm. Her outfit was beautifully pressed and there were little silk ruffles round her neck and cuffs. She was sitting patiently and, when Margery walked in, she smiled warmly at her one-time protégée. Hello, Margery, Mrs Hamilton said, in her rich and rather loud voice. Long-time no see.

Margery Darcy was paralysed with fear. She tried to scream, and couldn't.

Irene Hamilton had perished that Hallowe'en in 1979. She was like the others. The others who had turned green and rotten and insane during the course of that accursed cocktail do. And yet here she was.

'Come along, Margery. Won't you say hello?' Mrs Hamilton smiled, getting up and advancing on Margery.

Just as Margery at last found her voice…

In Reception, Martha jerked in response to the harsh screaming from the staff room. In an instant she vaulted the desk. There was a hubbub of noise from the other guests in Reception, but nobody followed her. It was as if that awful scream had struck all of them dumb. Martha raced bravely to the back room. She flung open the staff room door.

Margery Darcy was slumped on the lino like a broken doll, her body smothered with sticky green slime.

THE DOCTOR WAS HARD AT WORK IN THE TARDIS.
Bathed in the orange and green light of the control room, his face
was impassive as he read the dizzying reams of information on the
scanner. He had fed the slime sample to the instruments and now
they were confirming what he had suspected.

The green slime wasn't just something like pond slime. It was a
peculiar substance with unique properties. And it was alien.

He had thought as much. The Doctor had a very good nose for
these things.

He set the TARDIS to surveying the whole hotel and the ground
beneath it. An array of complicated maps and x-ray type pictures
whirled across the screen, examining the Hotel Splendide from
every angle.

And what was deep underneath those recent foundations?

The Doctor's eyebrows went up in disgust when he saw.

Bodies. Loads of dead bodies. There was a stratum of corpses
preserved in green slime. Deep under the hotel. Disturbed,
presumably, by the sinking of new foundations. Undetected at the
time by the builders... and now, forcing its way back to the surface
like ghoulish lava...

'Are you sure?' he muttered to the TARDIS.

Suddenly the Doctor clapped a hand to his forehead.
Bramlington-on-Sea. He had heard of this place, after all. Hadn't
there been... some kind of disaster? A terrible fire? Something
mysterious? Think think think!

He reached into his capacious memory for details, but there
was nothing more. He checked the TARDIS data banks and found
only a few pages in the local advertising paper. But there it was.
Hallowe'en 1979. Disaster struck. No survivors apart from one
trainee receptionist. Causes unknown. That's why it had
stuck in the Doctor's mind.

Should he grab Martha first?
He considered it for a

second, as his hands roved over the ragbag assortment of switches
and levers. No, leave her here in the present. A safe pair of hands
to fend off the monsters at this end.

In the meantime, the Doctor had an appointment way back in
the past... He grinned to himself as the TARDIS started up its
usual vworping brouhaha.

IRENE HAMILTON WAS JUST ABOUT ECSTATIC.

For years she had kept this motel afloat. Struggling through the
lean times. Bringing up her two children alone. The last few years
had been pretty tricky.

But now 1979 was coming to an end. A lovely, scintillating
optimism was washing over Irene. She put on her new frock,
and checked her hairdo was properly in place. Now she looked
splendid – even if she thought so herself – especially for a busy
motel manageress of fifty-something. She was ready to face her
beloved family and friends at the annual Hallowe'en cocktail party.

She left her suite of rooms at the back of the building and
headed up to the function room where, judging by the loud disco
music pounding through the walls, the party was already in full
swing.

Everything was working out nicely at the Ringroad Motel. Even
her no-good sister, Bunty, had returned to the fold, and promised
there would be no more trouble. Irene was giving her another
chance and, it turned out, Bunty was a fully-trained cordon bleu
chef! So that was good.

Irene passed through the kitchens – which were heaving and
clanging with activity – to check on preparations for tonight's
dinner. Bunty welcomed her warmly.

Bunty was even more glamorous than Irene.

'Darling!' they cried at each other,
and embraced.

Irene cast her eye over the preparations. 'Blue mashed potato, Bunty, dear? Green mayonnaise? Purple custard? Golden prawns?'

Bunty gave a carefree shrug. 'Simply food-colourings, Irene. It's a bit of Hallowe'en fun. Doesn't the spread look marvellous?'

Irene wouldn't openly criticise her sister. She knew how touchy Bunty could be. She didn't want to set her on the warpath. 'It's marvellous, darling.' What on earth would everyone make of Bunty's garish food?

'I'll see you upstairs, at the party,' she smiled thinly, and patted her sister's hand affectionately.

Bunty watched her go. Her eyes narrowed and the sisterly smile died on her face. She fetched out the tiny communications device from the front of her pinny. Dratted thing. How did it work again? Cecil had shown her, several times. But she was hopeless with technical gubbins. There. It was ringing. She popped into the store cupboard, where none of the other kitchen staff would see her talking into a device that didn't belong on this planet. If they saw, they might start asking awkward questions.

'Cecil?' Bunty knew he would be dressing for the party. He'd been in chalet seven, choosing which tie to wear. He had the most atrocious taste, Bunty had found. Colour coordination was not his forté.

'My love,' he said, in an unctuous tone. Bunty flushed. 'Is everything going according to plan?'

'Oh yes,' she said. 'Irene asked a few questions about the strange colours, but I just said I'd done it for effect. To make the buffet spooky for Hallowe'en.'

'Excellent,' he said. 'Bunty darling. I must go. Someone's knocking at my door, rather insistently…'

Bunty frowned as the futuristic communicator clicked off. Oh well. Best get on with transporting the buffet up to the function room. It was almost time to feed the masses…

…To feed them their just desserts.

Their viciously technicolour just desserts…

'HELLO?' DRAWLED CECIL LAZILY, AS HE OPENED THE fake wooden door of his chalet.

There was a tall man in a skinny suit grinning at him. 'Room service?' he asked hopefully.

'I never ordered anything,' Cecil said brusquely, and made to slam the door.

But now the lanky man seemed to be sniffing him, for some reason. 'Haven't seen any aliens about, have you? Intergalactic nasties?'

'I most certainly have not. I, sir, am a commercial traveller and I am here at the motel at the invitation of the Hamilton family.'

'Hmmmm,' the Doctor hummed. 'Are you sure you've not come across any alien life forms recently?' Then he clicked his fingers right in Cecil's face. 'I've got it! You're an alien! Disguised as human, right?'

The travelling salesman scowled. 'Nonsense.' He made a snap decision. He'd wear the pink tie with orange blobs. He fetched it up and slipped out of the room, locking it quickly behind him. The Doctor followed him all the way down the corridor, effortlessly keeping up with the furious Cecil.

'The thing is,' the Doctor said, 'I happen to know that there are scads of aliens hanging about at this point in Earth's history. A few spies and would-be invaders. A few left-overs from foiled invasions.' He grinned at Cecil warmly. 'I'm right, aren't I?'

Cecil stopped in his tracks. He held up his hands. 'Alright, alright. How did you know?'

'You've got green eyes.'

'So what? So do some human beings.'

'They don't have three of them. I can see the third one, just underneath your wig. Bad wig, by the way.'

Cecil cursed. He stomped onwards again. 'I'm going to this party. And you can't stop me.'

'I wonder what you are,' the Doctor taunted.

'Slitheen? Nah. Too slim. Zygon? Could be, I s'pose. Hiding your suckers well. Or…'

'I'm simply trying to live a quiet life here on Earth,' Cecil snapped.

'Got it!' the Doctor grinned. 'You're a –'

'I'm engaged to be married,' Cecil said. 'To a wonderful woman. Called Bunty.'

'You're a Kaftakkrofakian and you're up to no good,' said the Doctor sternly.

'Absolute poppycock,' Cecil retorted, having to shout now, because the party noise had become so fierce.

The Doctor pulled a face, and decided he was going to stick close by Cecil all evening.

Because, he knew, tonight was the night disaster would strike…

NOW MR PRESTON, THE HOTEL MANAGER, LOOKED even more appalled.

It was the end of a long and harrowing day at the Hotel

Splendide and the usually-reliable Margery Darcy was in his office, covered in that zombie gunk, gibbering like mad.

'It was her, I tell you,' Margery snapped. Her once-elegant hairdo was plastered to her forehead, and she looked about a hundred years old.

'Irene Hamilton died back in 1979,' Mr Preston said. 'You were the only survivor, remember?'

The actual events of that long-ago Hallowe'en were rather vague in Margery's memory. She had been in shock for quite a while following her escape from the inferno. Now this terrible encounter in the staff room was starting to revive some of the details and the sensations of that ghastly time… 'Irene is back,' she insisted. 'They are all back. They're coming out of the ground, even though we built a hotel on top of them… Their remains won't stay dead!'

The woman was plainly hysterical. Mr Preston leaned across his desk: 'Stop it! I won't have this in my hotel! You're ruining everything! You and your wild and horrible tales! And these… zombie things!'

Just at that moment the door flew open and Martha stumbled in. 'The Doctor's gone and left me here!'

'Your gentleman friend?' asked Mr Preston tersely. He didn't have any time to listen to romantic shenanigans. Not this evening.

'The TARDIS has gone,' Martha burst out. She could hardly believe it. 'I went out to the staff car park and he's… just vanished!'

Margery had become very still. A new, hopeful light was dawning in her eyes. 'Martha!' she burst out. 'The Doctor! I've seen him!'

Martha shrugged. 'I know. Earlier today. We were both in reception.'

Margery waved her hands. 'No! Not today. I mean ages ago. I scarcely know how it's possible… But… I have met him before. The apparition gave me such a bang on the head… my memory is coming back! And I remember! I met the Doctor – just as he is now – back then!'

'When?' Martha cried.

'1979!' Margery beamed, ghoulish in her coating of slime. 'At the Hallowe'en dinner dance at the Ringroad Motel!'

◆◆◆

BACK ON THAT PARTICULAR NIGHT IN 1979, WHEN THE Doctor sidled up to the bar to order some ginger pop, the woman serving really *was* a younger, sprightlier version of Margery Darcy.

The Doctor was keeping an eye on Cecil, as the alien breezed across the Function Room, through the sea of dancing bodies. Cecil examined the wildly colourful buffet laid out on the tables. He seemed pleased the guests were tucking in with gusto, blue eggs and golden prawns notwithstanding. But the Doctor also noticed that Cecil didn't touch anything. He didn't eat a morsel.

He watched Cecil greet a certain lady very enthusiastically. She was in a pinny and helping to serve the garish food.

'Who's the woman in all the make-up?' the Doctor asked the girl behind the counter.

Margery handed him a second pint of ginger pop. 'That's Bunty,' she scowled. 'She's Mrs Hamilton's wicked sister. But they've made up and Bunty's got the top job in the kitchens. She's not very popular. Do you fancy a boogie later, Doctor?'

'A what?' frowned the Doctor, only half-listening.

'A turn on the dance floor,' Margery said eagerly.

The Doctor nodded absently and moved off to examine the curious buffet.

He was poking at some violet vol-au-vents with his sonic screwdriver when the manageress, Irene Hamilton, caught him. She slapped his hand brusquely, frowned at him, and shoved a green profiterole into her mouth, before turning back to the guests she was chatting with.

The Doctor sniffed some silvery onion bhajis. They had that same, cloying, chemical smell he'd noticed back in the future hotel.

The buffet stank of zombie gunk. And that couldn't be good.

Cecil was standing there, arms folded, Bunty at his side. She wasn't eating anything, either. The Doctor glared at them. 'What are you two feeding everyone?'

'Just wait and see,' Cecil sneered. 'They will taste my bile! My alien spleen!'

The Doctor looked disgusted at this. He turned to Bunty: 'And what are you doing, knocking about with a rogue Kaftakkrofakian..?'

'He said he would show me the wonders of the universe,' Bunty sighed. 'And I said I'd go anywhere with him. So long as he helped me take revenge on everyone here at the Ringroad Motel. That's all I want: revenge. And poor Cecil wants the same, for the way his people were treated when they tried to invade the Earth. In the late Sixties, wasn't it, Cecil? He was left here alone, poor love.'

'Sssh, my dear,' Cecil told her. 'You don't have to tell this man everything.'

Bunty shrugged carelessly. 'Once they've started on the buffet, and the zombie virus takes a hold, they're all dead anyway, aren't they?'

The Doctor whirled about and started pushing people away from the buffet table. 'Don't eat the food! Don't touch the food!' A chorus of complaint rose up from the party-goers. 'I mean it!' the Doctor yelled. But he knew, deep in his hearts, that his words would have no effect.

History had already been written. He had seen the evidence. The poisoned buffet would do its hideous work that night.

Next thing he knew was being yanked onto the dance floor by Margery. She forced him to bop, right in the middle of a crowd of people dressed up as skeletons, monsters, vampires. All the while, though, the Doctor was looking perturbed. 'What is it?' she asked. 'And what was wrong with the buffet?'

'You didn't touch any of it, did you, Margery?'

She grimaced. 'I wouldn't touch anything that Bunty had made. And I've been behind the bar all night… why?'

'Good,' he said. 'Look. We're going to slip outside in a second, before…'

But just as Baccara started singing 'Yes Sir, I Can Boogie', the alien poison was manifesting its effects. The stink of alien slime was in the smoky air. The Doctor turned to see a few green faces in the crowd. They weren't just bilious. Their very flesh was changing and they were screaming…

Shrieks of alarm went up. Crashes of furniture. Howls of horror. Bodies were jerking spasmodically on the lit-up dance floor.

'Zombies!' the Doctor hissed, in Margery's ear. 'Poisoned by the nibbles. Come on!'

Margery could only stare, appalled, as people she knew socially were transformed into slavering beasts, attacking each other in the Function Room. All of them had become rabid, insane. She saw Irene the manageress, bright green and …what was she whirling triumphantly around her head..? A severed green arm. Ripped from the body of one of her shareholders. Margery screamed.

'Come on!' the Doctor insisted, bundling her out of the room.

Just as there was a series of small explosions. Sparks and flames were sputtering out of the DJ's equipment as green slime wormed its way into the workings.

That's where the fire started, the Doctor realised. Now the flames were spreading to the heavy velvet curtains and the paper streamers.

In a matter of minutes the whole place would be up…

'We can't just leave them all!' yelled Margery, as they ran through the corridors of the motel.

'We have to,' said the Doctor grimly. 'It's all history now…'

As they ran across the empty reception area Cecil and Bunty stepped out from the shadows, barring their way to the door.

'There will be no survivors to tell the tale,' Cecil said, murderously.

Already the place was filling up with smoke and the smell of zombie gunk.

'You can't stop us,' said the Doctor, furious.

'Let's just see about that,' said Cecil, striding towards him menacingly…

'AND THEN WHAT HAPPENED?' GASPED MARTHA.

In the present, Margery Darcy was sipping a sugary mug of tea and telling the tale as it unfolded again in her memory. 'Well, then there was the most almighty punch-up. Even with all the smoke and the fire alarms going off, and the flames starting to spread to Reception. Even with all the screams of the newly-made zombies howling through the motel… the Doctor and Cecil were rolling about on the carpet having a terrible fight. And meanwhile, I was relishing the chance of smacking that show-off Bunty in the chops. Ooh, it was a terrible fight to the death.'

'The death!' cried Mr Preston, alarmed. He was shocked to hear all about the final moments of the Ringroad Motel, and he was looking at Margery Darcy with new eyes.

'Anyway, I knocked Bunty out cold with the reservations folder. And then I saw that the Doctor had Cecil in a headlock. 'How do we reverse the effects of the alien gloop?' he was shouting. 'What's the antidote to the zombie poison?' And then that Cecil was cursing: 'It's too late! It's done its work!' And the Doctor yelled again, right down his ear: 'Give me the antidote anyway!''

Martha was on her feet. 'And did he?'

'I- I think so,' Margery said. 'Next thing I remember… we were standing out in the freezing night.

By the side of the ringroad and it was pitch black. Apart from the Motel, which was spewing flames everywhere. I think I'd gone into shock, dragging Bunty's unconscious body. And… yes! Cecil was saying, 'You can't use it now!'… But the Doctor took some kind of flask off him anyway. And then… I remember the Doctor kissing me goodbye. And telling me to forget everything… about Hallowe'en 1979… And then he… climbed into some sort of… blue box. And was gone!' Margery blinked and swallowed the last of her tea. 'And I *did* forget, didn't I?'

Mr Preston stared at her. 'What a preposterous tale..!'

'Sssh,' said Martha sharply, listening hard.

A few papers flew off Mr Preston's desk. Was there a breeze?

And then a very familiar wheezing, groaning noise shattered the silence.

'Doctor!' Martha shouted, as the TARDIS doors shot open. 'We know where you've been! 1979!'

The Doctor grinned ruefully. He looked a bit roughed-up and smoke-damaged, after his scrap in the motel reception. But he held up a flask triumphantly. 'Antidote for the alien zombie gloop!' he sighed. 'I got it! I knew there had to be one. Cecil and his girlfriend would want insurance, in case they were affected by the poison they unleashed here. I had to really wrestle with him to get it, though. Hullo, Martha.' He patted her on the back and sank heavily into an office chair. He tossed the precious bottle to Mr Preston, who caught it rather less than deftly and looked very worried. 'This should put paid to your zombie visitors forever. They're in a huge cavern, way beneath the foundations. Not a very sensible place to build a luxury hotel, by the way.'

Now Margery was staring at the Doctor. 'You saved my life! All those years ago!'

He winked at her rakishly. 'Wotcha, Margery. You been here all this time?'

'Where are Cecil… and Bunty?' Martha asked. 'Still in 1979?'

'Nope,' said the Doctor carelessly. 'I made him a bargain. I'd take him back to his home world, but only if he gave me the antidote and took Bunty home with him.'

'Good!' Margery said.

'Of course, he agreed. He was expecting a hero's welcome, back on old planet Kaftakkrofakkia…,' the Doctor smiled. 'But there's been a regime change. Poor old Cecil's standing trial as we speak. And Bunty's not so chuffed to be on another world. She fell for a charming travelling salesman. Not a flesh-eating insectoid serving a life-sentence… You should have seen him shouting "Wait for me, Bunty!" from the dock. Only Bunty's not looking so keen anymore.'

'Well, I'm glad Bunty's got her comeuppance at last,' Margery said firmly.

The Doctor laughed, and turned to frown at Mr Preston. 'What are you waiting for? I've been to a lot of trouble to sort your problems out! Go and get on with it! De-zombify your Splendide Hotel!' He frowned at Margery suddenly. 'Best give Margery a swig of the antidote first, eh? She's covered in toxic slime. We don't want her going on the rampage.'

Margery looked alarmed, and took a hesitant swig of the strange medicine.

'All in a day's work, eh, Doctor?' Martha laughed.

'Hmm,' said the Doctor, putting his feet up. 'You know, I'm quite fond of 1979, in a funny kind of way. We should have a weekend there some time, Martha. Mind you, the food is absolutely diabolical.'

THE END

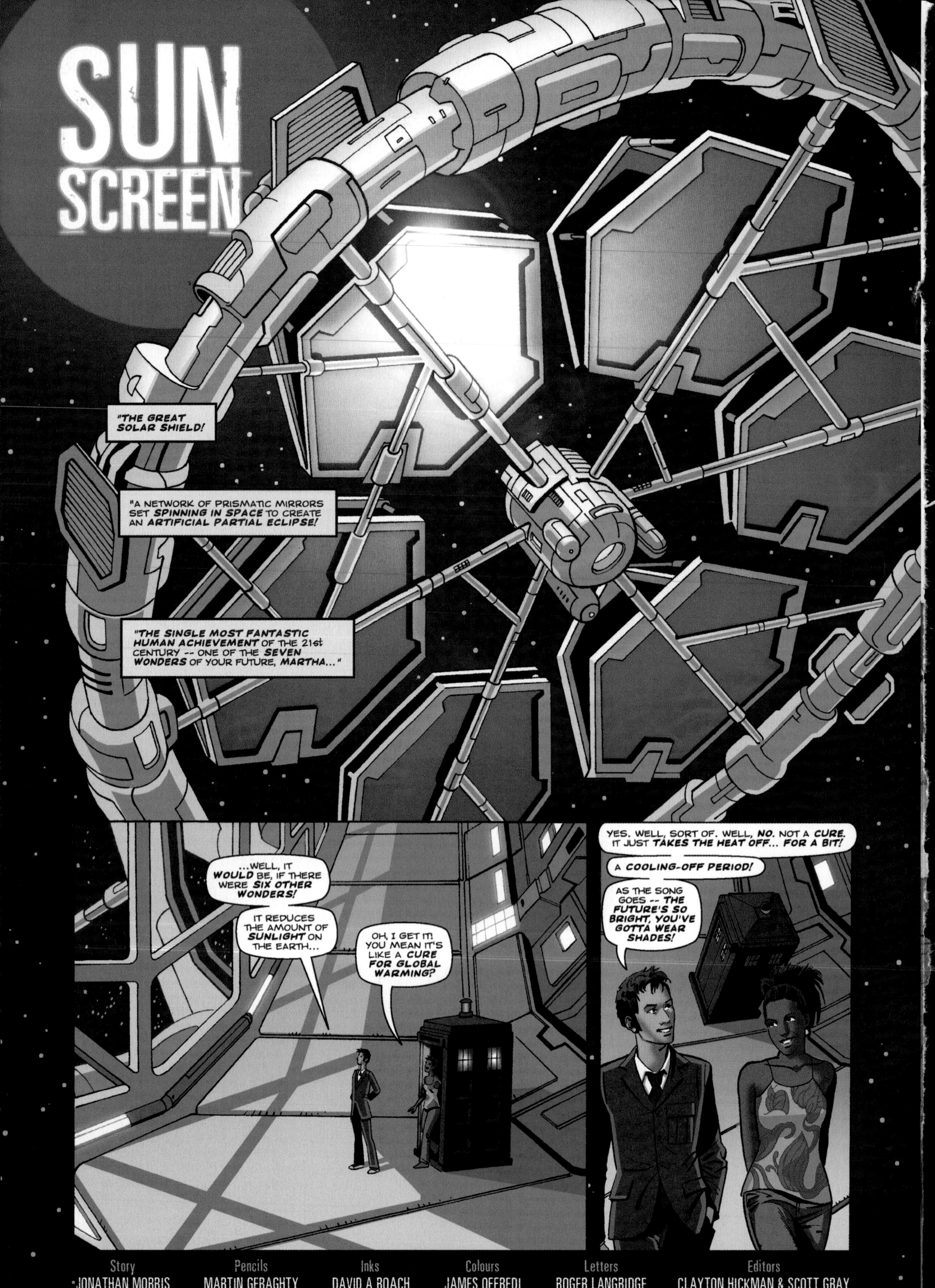

SUN SCREEN

"THE GREAT SOLAR SHIELD!

"A NETWORK OF PRISMATIC MIRRORS SET *SPINNING IN SPACE* TO CREATE AN *ARTIFICIAL PARTIAL ECLIPSE!*

"THE *SINGLE MOST FANTASTIC HUMAN ACHIEVEMENT* OF THE 21st CENTURY -- ONE OF THE *SEVEN WONDERS* OF YOUR FUTURE, *MARTHA...*"

...WELL, IT *WOULD* BE, IF THERE WERE *SIX OTHER WONDERS!*

IT REDUCES THE AMOUNT OF *SUNLIGHT* ON THE EARTH...

OH, I GET IT! YOU MEAN IT'S LIKE A *CURE* FOR *GLOBAL WARMING?*

YES. WELL, SORT OF. WELL, *NO.* NOT A *CURE.* IT JUST *TAKES THE HEAT OFF...* FOR A BIT!

A *COOLING-OFF PERIOD!*

AS THE SONG GOES -- THE *FUTURE'S SO BRIGHT, YOU'VE GOTTA WEAR SHADES!*

Story
JONATHAN MORRIS

Pencils
MARTIN GERAGHTY

Inks
DAVID A ROACH

Colours
JAMES OFFREDI

Letters
ROGER LANGRIDGE

Editors
CLAYTON HICKMAN & SCOTT GRAY

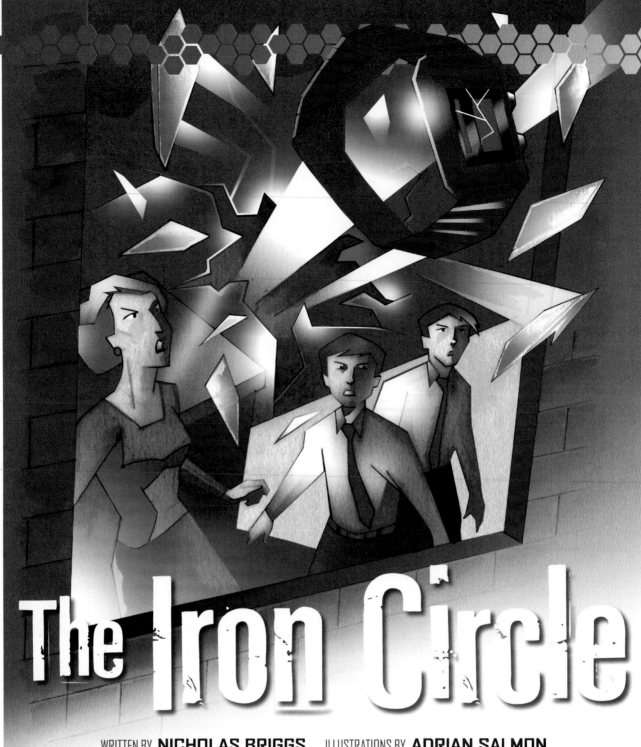

The Iron Circle

WRITTEN BY **NICHOLAS BRIGGS**   ILLUSTRATIONS BY **ADRIAN SALMON**

BEING A MAINLANDER ON THE ISLE OF WIGHT WAS
proving to be more of a problem for nine-year-old Ben than he'd
ever imagined. Dad's job had already uprooted him from a rural
Southampton suburb and planted him in the pongy brewery town of
Burton-upon-Trent; but the slightly Brummy-sounding school kids
there had welcomed what they had mistakenly thought was a 'posh
kid' with genuinely friendly curiosity. However, here he was, in the
third month of his time on this rough little diamond-shaped piece of
land off the south coast of England… and he was still the outsider.
He had been surrounded by the entire school in the playground on his
first day and been relentlessly chanted at. Things had not significantly
improved since then. Mysteriously put in a remedial class for English
– his best subject – and a bewilderingly algebraic class for Maths, Ben
had concluded that the teachers also inexplicably hated him as much
as his fellow pupils did.

Today was the last straw. Dragged into a darkened cloakroom by
a spindly, vicious-looking, oddly reptilian boy called Timothy, he had
been pushed around and verbally abused. Ben was not a fighter, and
he was preparing himself for a beating, when suddenly, his left arm
was thrown against a rack of coats by some inexplicable, irresistible
force. *Kerchink!* His wristwatch's face was broken. His lovely watch,

bought for him by his lovely Mum and Dad. That was it. Something
snapped inside him and almost without thinking, he grabbed
Timothy's arm and marched him to the headmistress's office, hardly
noticing the insistent tugging from his watch. Strangely, the silver-
haired, rather elegant Mrs Collis seemed not to believe Ben's claims of
being bullied, concentrating on the issue of how rude it was for Ben to
frogmarch anyone into her office. When he offered his watch as proof
of the heinous assault, things took a turn for the distinctly weird…

No sooner was the watch off his wrist than it started to float away
from Ben's grasp and into mid-air. Mrs Collis immediately seemed
to blame Ben for this, glaring at him. More proof of the oddness of
mainlanders, Ben imagined her thinking. And to make matters worse,
the watch shot straight out of the window, showering them with glass.

And as the watch flew skywards, it left behind it a whole
headmistress's study full of anger and confusion.

MARTHA WAS SURE THAT SOMETHING HAD MOVED ON
the TARDIS console… and the funny thing was that the Doctor was
on the other side of the control room, soldering a broken bit of floor
grating back into place.

The soldering stopped. The Doctor looked round.

'Did you see that?' asked Martha.

'Er... not sure,' said the Doctor. 'Maybe.'

A couple of tiny, slightly loose switches wiggled in their mountings. In an instant, the Doctor was by Martha's side, staring at the switches. She gave him an 'Aren't you going to do something about that?' sort of a look. The Doctor shrugged.

'Probably nothing,' he said, about to turn back to his soldering. Then, all of a sudden, the whole TARDIS seemed to... wobble a bit.

'Okay, probably something,' said the Doctor, returning to the console and pulling the screen round to face him. 'Ohhh!' he suddenly blurted out, as if that explained everything. Then he just stared at the screen for a while.

'Yeah, well, that explains it,' laughed Martha, determined not to be wound up by the Doctor's unique brand of eccentricity.

'Earth, 1973... er... ish,' said the Doctor.

'Oh yeah. It's all clear to me now. Thanks for sorting that out,' she said, nudging him in the ribs.

And then a small, metal wristwatch shot through one side of the control room, circled the control column and shot back out through the wall on the other side. No sign of entry. No sign of exit.

'Now *that*,' said the Doctor, 'is not supposed to happen.'

OLD MICK BURNS WAS ON HIS WAY UP ON AN industrial scissor-lift, checking for rust on an electricity pylon just outside Ventnor, on the Isle of Wight. He gazed around as the machinery whined noisily. No one much about; just cows in a field and distant, countryside traffic. In contravention of Health and Safety regulations, his mate Dave Connell had gone off to the local garage to get them both a can of 'fizzy stuff', as Dave had described it. Mick was happy. I mean, what could go wrong with an industrial scissor lift alongside a pylon?

Mick soon found out.

With a worrying *thwack*, something broke in the scissor-lift's engine. A belt pinged out, just missing the ear of a nearby cow. The cow turned and mooed in annoyance, but when it saw what was actually going on, it ran for its life.

As the lift started bumping downwards onto itself, hissing almost in irritation, Mick saw what was happening too. The pylon was starting to move. But it wasn't falling or sliding. It was picking its own 'legs' up and starting to walk.

Iron groaned and creaked, but miraculously did not break as the pylon lumbered forward. There was the faint smell of ozone around the metal structure and a slight fizzing sound.

Mick resisted the temptation to reach out and touch the pylon. He had remembered at least some of his Health and Safety training. But he had more pressing problems. The scissor-lift was starting to move too, and in the same direction as the pylon.

'Mick!'

Mick turned round to see Dave approaching with two cans of fizzy stuff. He could understand why his mate looked so distressed. It's not every day you see a pylon going for a walk, after all. But then Mick noticed that Dave was pointing further afield than just his misbehaving pylon and scissor-lift. As far as you could see, right across the Isle of Wight, pylons were on the move, all of them heading due west. And all around them, electrical cables were twanging and snapping, sizzling and sparking. Cows were running. Cars were hooting their horns, screeching to a halt.

And as Mick crashed to the ground, having leapt to safety from his wayward scissor-lift just in time to see it do a somersault and tumble off to catch up with the pylon, he could see that now the cars were also heading west. Crashing through hedges and fences, smashing into each other or anyone who might dare to get in their way, cars, lorries and

one rather old milk float were being drawn onto the pylons' course.

THE DOCTOR WAS STRUGGLING TO MATERIALISE THE TARDIS. He'd located something significant in Southern England in 1973 as they were passing close to it in the vortex. He'd also ascertained that the floating watch had come from that time and place

as well. But when he had set about the routine operation of landing the TARDIS there, a significant number of the console's controls had started to take on a life of their own.

A thrum of horrible uncertainty ran down the column into the console. The Doctor, already spreading his hands, arms and feet over several control panels nodded for Martha to steady yet another rattling switch. She stretched to reach it, trying not to let go of the lever bracket she was already holding onto. It was like they were playing an especially uncomfortable game of Twister on the console.

Martha's hand slapped down on the switch. Beneath her palm, it wriggled furiously, scratching at her skin. Another thrum shot down the glass column, but this time it sustained like a relentless, discordant attack on piano wires. And the sound was growing.

'Just in case you thought I knew what was going on!' yelled the Doctor over the terrible racket, 'I don't! Sorry! I'd like to be more reassuring, but there you are!'

'Are we gonna fall to bits?' asked Martha, wincing at the increasing pain of the switch now digging into her palm.

'If we can just lock the controls into the position I've put them in, we should land!' shouted the Doctor. 'The trouble is, they're–!'

'I know!' cried Martha. 'What's got into them?'

Then the familiar groaning of materialisation started to sound. The Doctor and Martha cocked their ears and smiled as if at the arrival of an old friend.

'So... that's all right, isn't it?' asked Martha, hopefully.

'Very nearly!' said the Doctor, over the continuing din. 'It's going to be slow and we may be a bit off target!'

HIGH ABOVE TENNYSON DOWNS ON THE ISLE OF WIGHT, in the summer of 1973, the TARDIS crackled into existence up in the wispy-clouded blue sky. A few seagulls screeched and ducked as the glowing box twirled quickly downwards, towards the green grass of the cliff-tops. The groaning engine sound, slightly laboured at the best of times, was almost choking and coughing.

Inside, the Doctor was just beginning to think he had everything under control when, *bong*, a huge reverberation rumbled through the control room. The force of it threw Martha and the Doctor right off the console.

As they crashed to the floor, the TARDIS settled at last and silence descended.

Rubbing his head and squinting up at the column, the Doctor said, 'Well done, old girl. You made it.'

'Did we hit something?' asked Martha, staggering to her feet.

'Er... you know, I think we did,' said the Doctor. 'I wonder what.'

'COULD IT HAVE BEEN THAT?' ASKED MARTHA AS SHE exited the TARDIS.

They were both out on the soft grass now; only a slight breeze ruffling their hair.

'What, Lord Tennyson's monument? Nah, I don't think so,' said the Doctor. 'It's just granite, I think. If we'd hit that, it'd be in bits now. Anyway, we were probably further up in the sky when we hit whatever it was.'

He strode round the monument. A stone monolith, engraved with commemorative inscriptions.

'Y'know,' continued the Doctor, with a smile, 'I remember someone

telling me that's what killed him.'

'Who?' asked Martha, a little distracted.

'Alfred Lord Tennyson. What a poet. They said he died carrying this monument all the way up here,' he laughed, then his face straightened. 'Not funny, of course. Not true, either.'

'Er… I wasn't talking about that monument,' said Martha.

'Mm?' the Doctor turned, and his expression changed. 'Yeah, funny how you can miss things when you think you know the territory.'

Hands thrust in the pockets of his comfortable, long coat, the Doctor strode towards something else pointing skywards on Tennyson Downs. It was large, metallic-looking and it completely dwarfed the old poet's monument.

'Do you think that's what we hit?' asked Martha.

'Yeah… Yeah, I think there's a good chance of that,' said the Doctor, staring at a considerable dent in the large, metallic-looking thing.

'And I take it this *thing* wasn't here last time you visited,' offered Martha.

'Nope,' he said, squinting and hoping inspiration would suddenly hit him. But it didn't. 'I give up,' he said, simply, 'What is it?'

Towering above them was an oddly shaped, metallic structure, which must have been all of five hundred feet tall. The Doctor and Martha simply stared at it.

'Lovely day for it,' muttered the Doctor.

'What, staring at a big metal thingy?' asked Martha. 'Hang on, is that a beak?'

'What? Oh… yeah, could be,' said the Doctor.

The trouble was that it was difficult to make out the precise shape of anything in the structure. It seemed to give the distinct impression that it was a statue of some kind of life-form, but just when a feature seemed discernable, several other shapes would catch the summer sun and dispel the impression altogether.

'It's sort of… defying classification, isn't it?' said Martha. She rubbed her jaw.

The Doctor noticed, asking, 'You all right?'

'Er…' Martha wiggled her jaw a little, testing a feeling that had just started. 'I think I'm getting tooth-ache.'

'I might have some oil of cloves somewhere,' said the Doctor, patting his pockets. Then he spotted something just to the left of the dent that he'd presumed had been left by the impact of the TARDIS. 'Is that a watch?'

YOUNG BEN WAS JUST BEING MARCHED OUT OF SCHOOL to meet his mother at the gates. He was being sent home for causing disruptive behaviour and smashing the headmistress's window. Ben had just about given up trying to explain that his watch had taken on a life of its own. No one seemed to believe him. But luckily for Ben, his worries were about to become supremely irrelevant.

As he reached the main door of the school, he began to hear a sound he'd never actually heard before. But when he turned to discover the source, it struck him how appropriate the cacophony was for the unbelievable sight he was witnessing.

All the cutlery from the school dining hall was flying down the corridor towards him. Almost without thinking, Ben flung himself out of the school, pushing his waiting mum to the ground to protect her, then buried his head in the gravel path.

The cutlery shot overhead, jingling and jangling, then swooped upwards into the sky like synchronized starlings. He and his mum looked up in disbelief, just in time to see Mrs Collis flailing to avoid a squadron of formation-flying metal music stands. Fifteen triangles followed, opting to exit through the windows, showering glass all around.

If they hadn't been ducking down, Ben and his mum would have

noticed the approaching pylons and the flying cars. Mrs Collis saw them though, and immediately wished she hadn't.

'SAY AHHHH,' SAID THE DOCTOR, LOOKING INTO Martha's mouth.

'Ahhh,' she obliged. But then her 'ahhh' turned into an 'Aaaargh!' as she felt a sharp, wincing pain.

Staring intensely into Martha's mouth, the Doctor's expression suddenly became very serious indeed.

'Ot issit?' Martha managed to say, her mouth still open.

The Doctor's eyebrows arched and his eyes narrowed in disbelief. Martha yelped in pain again, and the Doctor just managed to dodge in time as something hard and dark flew out of her mouth.

Clutching her jaw, Martha gingerly checked her mouth with a finger. The Doctor was holding onto her, more out of sympathy than anything else.

'I think… I think,' she began in disbelief, 'I think I… Ow!'

'Lost your filling!' said the Doctor.

'Yeah,' she agreed. 'How did that happen?'

The Doctor looked straight past her.

'Oh no,' he said, 'How did *that* happen?'

Martha spun round. If she hadn't been holding her jaw, it surely would have dropped. Coming towards them across the brow of the Compton cliffs that lead down into Freshwater Bay, just below the Downs on which the Doctor and Martha were standing, was an insane-looking army of cacophonous, misshapen metal. Cars tumbling, cutlery swooping, music stands scything and in the centre of it all, the giant, spindly forms of electricity pylons striding on their four 'feet'.

'Aw, is that one of those old milk floats down there?' asked the Doctor, with some affection, squinting through the moving debris. 'You know, the three-wheeler kind that ran on a battery and could only go at–'

'Yeah, probably, but what about the rest of it?' interrupted Martha, now so gob-smacked that she'd forgotten about her gob-agony. 'And how come the pylons are walking?'

Fizzes of electrical sparking energy sizzled on the surfaces of the pylons as they made their impossible, striding movements.

'Multi-molecular manipulation,' muttered the Doctor, largely to himself.

'That thing!' Martha pointed to the giant, metal structure behind them. 'It's… a magnet or something! It's attracting metal. That watch, my filling and now… well, all that stuff! Why?'

The Doctor didn't reply, seemingly mesmerised by the oncoming horde.

'Actually,' continued Martha, 'forget the

"why" – it's coming this way and it's going to, I dunno, crush us or something!'

She tugged at the Doctor's arm. He resisted, calmly staring down at the sea of metal. 'Hang on. We've got a few minutes yet.'

'Okaaay,' said Martha, trying to calm down. Staring ahead, she could see that the metal mass was now about to enter a small, seaside town. 'And what was it you were saying… multiple-molecules or something?'

The Doctor took out his sonic screwdriver, holding on tightly just in case, clicked its switch and took a few readings. 'Some sort of manipulation of the atomic structure of–'

'Doctor, what about all the people down there?' pleaded Martha.

Suddenly, the Doctor was alive with activity. He turned and ran. Martha thought he would head for the TARDIS, but he veered round it and went straight to the base of the metal structure. Then, with all his might, he hammered on it.

'Hello! Hello! Come in! This is the Doctor calling!' he yelled at the top of his voice.

'Er, is that going to work?' asked Martha. 'Statues don't usually–'

'It isn't a statue!' said the Doctor, eyes ablaze. 'It's manipulating the atomic structure of those objects. That takes pretty impressive science and pretty impressive science takes whopping great intelligence. And whopping great intelligence means language and language means the TARDIS's telepathic circuits can interpret it, so *come on and answer me!*' he suddenly yelled, slapping the structure again, in time to his words.

By this time, Martha was by the Doctor's side, and she heard the sound of his voice actually reverberate within the structure, like his words had somehow soaked through the surface and were now bouncing around inside. They waited. But there was no reply, except…

The oncoming metal army had been making one hell of a noise during its advance. And suddenly, Martha noticed, that noise had gone.

The Doctor had clearly noticed too, and the two of them turned together. Down below, in the bay, the metal army had stopped, as if it had suddenly been frozen stiff. Pylons were poised in mid-step. Cars were upended in mid-tumble. Cutlery hovered in mid-air.

'So, what is it? Is it a spaceship? Are there people in there? And – what? They heard you?' asked Martha, not believing for a second that the mass of frozen metal would stay still for long.

'No, not a spaceship,' said the Doctor. 'I think… Did you see that?'

Martha hadn't seen anything. The Doctor was staring at the structure, midway up. She followed his gaze. There was nothing there. The Doctor seemed tense, like a birdwatcher who'd glimpsed a rare breed and was scared he would never see it again.

'I think,' the Doctor whispered, 'I saw a… a blink.'

'A blink?' whispered Martha.

And there it was. A thin layer of metal seemed to… blink. Thin and oval-shaped, with something dark and glistening underneath. And again.

And then there was a deep rumble. Martha checked back to see if the metal army had started to move again, but it was quite still. And the rumble continued, louder and louder and louder until she thought it might vibrate all her teeth out, let alone her one filling.

'*What…?*' the rumble had suddenly formed into a voice. Now there was silence.

The Doctor and Martha exchanged looks. He smiled and she caught his smile.

'It's talking,' said Martha, amazed. The Doctor was clearly amused by her amazement.

She wondered if that was one of the reasons he travelled with human beings, just to capture their amazement and marvel at it. Then it struck her that the creature had only spoken one word.

'What?' asked Martha of the creature, 'You said "what?". What does "what" mean?

Another rumble started to build. As harsh and as loud and as long as the first. And just as abruptly, the rumbled resolve into...

'...time do you call this?' said the rumbling voice.

'Oh my god, we've woken it up. That's what my Dad always says!' said Martha.

'Er, 1973, Earth time,' said the Doctor, as clearly as he could. 'What are you doing here, if you don't mind my asking?'

Then there was a long silence. The Doctor tapped the creature.

'Hello! Wake up!' he shouted. 'Please?'

He and Martha looked hard for any signs of blinking. Any sign that the creature might wake up... Martha caught sight of the wristwatch

the Doctor had seen earlier, stuck to one of the bumps high above them. But just as her eyes chanced upon it, the shape of the watch started to blur into the main body of the creature. She quickly pointed it out to the Doctor.

'Absorption of matter,' murmured the Doctor, fascinated.

Then there was another flicking of a metal eyelid. Then, further up the creature, another flicking... Then, slightly to the left, another...

'Three eyes?' asked Martha.

'And that's just on this side,' said the Doctor. Then he turned his attention to the creature. 'Are you awake again? You just absorbed some metal. Is that giving you energy?'

A rumble started again. The Doctor and Martha stood, waiting for more vocal communication. At last, they would have some answers. But then, the rumble diminished again and faded to nothing.

'What was that?' asked Martha, a little dismissively. 'A metal snore?'

The Doctor flinched as a tiny, short, unpleasant screeching sound lanced across the bay towards them. It was metal moving, ever so slightly... but it *was* moving.

'We distracted it from its... I dunno, feeding mode, maybe,' he theorised, agitatedly. 'Now it's nodding off again, it'll start to bring all that stuff towards it again.'

'To absorb. Like it did the watch. Well, we need to feed it. Get its attention. Wake it up,' said Martha.

The Doctor raised a single finger of intense agreement and approval, almost as if he might suddenly say, 'By Jove, I think she's got it!'. But he never said that sort of thing. Instead, he dived into the TARDIS, the doors and his coat tails flapping behind him.

Another screech came from across the bay. Martha turned to look at the mass of poised metal. She couldn't see any movement, but she could almost feel the vibration that must be building up. Then she looked down at the helpless little coastal town in the path of the spiky, destructive mass. She could just make out a man on a bicycle who had caught sight of it all. He fell off his bike, then staggered off down the street, too confused to cry out.

'You can't let all that metal squash that town! You can't do that! It'd be mass murder!' shouted Martha, not expecting a reply from the statue, but hoping that her words might at least keep this strange creature partially awake. Then a thought occurred to her. How far had all that metal come? And what terrible damage had it wrought on the way?

At that moment, the Doctor emerged from the TARDIS carrying a mass of switches and levers.

'What are you doing?' asked Martha. 'They're not–?'

'Yep! They're all the switches and levers and brackets off the console that were rattling,' beamed the Doctor.

'But, you can't–'

'These are all the switches and levers and brackets that have tiny traces of Earth minerals in them. Not all of them do. But some of them do, and this thing obviously likes minerals like the ones that can be found on Earth. Hence all that lot!' he said gesturing across the bay.

Then suddenly, and in a rather balletic fashion, the vast mass of metal that had been so precariously poised across the bay, leapt gently into the air, as if bounding like an antelope, and landed at the foot of Tennyson Downs.

At that moment, all the switches and levers gathered in the Doctor's arms, shot straight from his grasp and onto the surface of the creature. As they slowly merged into the metal skin, a huge rumble started and the three eyes flickered again.

'*I am being careful, you know,*' said the deep, rumbling voice.

'You mean, you're not killing anyone?' asked Martha.

Another rumble. '*You almost sound disappointed,*' said the creature.

'No, no, it's just that–'

'*I don't want any of that fleshy stuff. It's horrible. Clogs up my arteries,*' it rumbled.

'Glad to hear it,' said the Doctor. 'The trouble is, you can't just come to this planet and nick all their metal.'

There was a kind of 'considering' rumble. But no speech was forthcoming.

'At least it's not arguing with you,' commented Martha.

'*You're a bit stupid, aren't you?*' it suddenly rumbled.

The Doctor looked offended.

It continued. '*Why would I want all the metal? I'd burst. I just need enough to replenish my deficiency.*'

'So… you really do… *eat* it?' asked Martha.

'It's more like refuelling at a petrol station,' whispered the Doctor to Martha.

'*No, it's eating,*' rumbled the creature. '*Who are you, anyway?*'

'Oh, well, I'm the Doctor and this is Martha. Your, er, dietary needs pulled us down here,' said the Doctor, trying to be as polite as possible. 'So, there's a limit to the amount you need, is there?'

'*I usually just mark out a small, circular area, then draw everything in,*' explained the huge, rumbling voice.

'An iron circle…' the Doctor mused to himself. Then, aloud, he said, 'Anything unlucky enough to get in your way gets sucked in, does it?'

'*I sense disapproval,*' rumbled the creature. '*What do you eat when you get hungry?*'

The Doctor and Martha did a bit of simultaneous thinking. The slab of metal gave off what Martha imagined was a somewhat smug resonance; or maybe that was just the result of the vague but uncomfortable feelings of guilt welling up in her.

She turned to the Doctor. 'It's about to tell us we should all be vegetarians, isn't it? That we eat living things and that at least he only eats bits of metal and makes sure he doesn't kill anyone in the process.'

The Doctor tickled the back of his ear, awkwardly. 'Er… yeah, yeah, I think he might be about to say something like that, yeah.' He turned to the metal creature, trying to locate one of the eyes. Seven immediately opened, and although there was no clearly defined pupil, there could be no doubt that those eyes were all staring at the Doctor and Martha.

A rumble began. '*Plants are alive as well, you know,*' it said. '*Isn't destruction in the nature of creation and death in the nature of life?*'

'That's very deep,' said the Doctor.

'That was a bit flip,' said Martha.

The Doctor moved very close to the living metal. 'I didn't catch your name,' he said, gently.

'*I didn't give it,*' rumbled the creature.

'Yeah, right, I see what's happening here. You're kind of claiming the moral high ground, aren't you? In your little iron circle of feeding here, you're claiming that you're better than us because you feed on stuff that isn't alive. Am I right?'

'*I don't claim anything. I'm just hungry… and thank you for your switches and levers,*' it rumbled.

'You're welcome,' said the Doctor. Martha wondered if he'd meant to say it in such a high voice. She was fairly certain the Doctor was squirming a bit. She beckoned him back to her side.

'So, no one's been hurt and the damage has already been done,' she said, pointing over her shoulder to the still poised metal mass.

The Doctor turned and looked at the pylons and the cars and all the other glistening, twisted, battered metal before him. 'And they've still got all their plastic and stuff, haven't they?'

There was another rumble. '*Your switches and levers have given me just enough energy to move on and find another place, if that's what you really want,*' the creature said.

'But what damage would you do there? Wherever "there" might end up being?' asked the Doctor. He turned to Martha again. He seemed to be seeking her opinion.

'Maybe we could, you know, strike a deal. He could just eat half of it,' she suggested. The Doctor was clearly thinking it over. But the creature had overheard.

'*I would be happy with that "deal",*' it said.

'Yeah, but,' mused the Doctor, "even if half of all that metal was just left lying around up here, it'd cause… well, a lot of kerfuffle frankly,' said the Doctor. 'Questions would be asked. There'd be government scientists crawling all over it, state of emergency declared. Better there's just the mystery of the vanishing metal. They'll probably just blame it on… I dunno, whatever they're currently blaming everything on.'

'*So I take the lot?*' asked the creature, slightly wearily, as if it was contemplating doing a favour for a rather irritating child. Anything for a quiet life…

The Doctor looked at the metal mass, to Martha, to the creature, then back to the mass. Martha found she couldn't really raise an objection. The Doctor moved confidentially close to the creature and muttered something.

'What are you saying?' asked Martha.

'Run!' shouted the Doctor, grabbing her arm and dragging her towards the TARDIS.

As they pounded across the grass towards the doors, Martha could hear the crashing and grinding of the metal mass beginning to move. She dared not look back until she knew she was safe.

They entered the TARDIS and she glanced over her shoulder just as the Doctor was slamming the doors shut. She caught a glimpse of all that metal, so close and so vicious-looking that it seemed to make her heart flutter in her throat. It crossed her mind that this was a sight she would never forget, but she knew she'd already seen far too many of those to be sure.

The Doctor dashed to the console, but where half of the switches, levers and brackets had been, there were now only twisted bits of cable and broken mountings. He played his hands over them helplessly.

'Ooops,' he said. Then he relaxed. 'Don't worry, the TARDIS is indestructible.'

And at that moment, there was a huge crash, as the metal mass presumably tumbled down on the TARDIS on its way into the metal creature. Martha wondered if the Doctor was sure about this indestructibility thing, and then she saw how tightly he had his fingers crossed…

Suddenly, everything was quiet.

'It's absorbed all that metal, hasn't it?' asked Martha.

'Bon appetite!' said the Doctor, with a broad smile.

THAT EVENING, THE DOCTOR AND MARTHA STROLLED down towards Freshwater. There wasn't much going on. They picked up a local newspaper. Martha read it over the Doctor's shoulder. There was a third-place story about 'hooligans' from the pop festival playing a prank and stealing pylons. There was also a photograph of a milkman standing next to his battered, battery-operated milk float, the three-wheeler kind.

'You asked that creature to save the milk van, didn't you?' grinned Martha.

The Doctor seemed not to hear her. He quickly flicked the pages of the newspaper. There was also a photograph of a London police box on Tennyson Downs. More 'hooligan' pranks, a pompously written piece seemed to imply.

'We'd better go and finish fixing the console,' said the Doctor.

'And then maybe we could find a planet with really good dentists,' winced Martha, rubbing her jaw.

A ball rolled up to them, and a group of nearby kids called over, waving for them to return it. The Doctor grinned and kicked it expertly back to them.

Ben stopped the ball and gave a thumbs-up to the skinny man in the big coat. Then he turned back to the group of boys. His new friends, he reminded himself. It was amazing how interested they'd been in his story of deadly flying cutlery, although it was smashing the headmistress's window that seemed to have impressed them the most.

As the game began again in earnest, Ben looked around, over the green hills, towards the sparkling sea beyond, and wondered whether the Isle of Wight was such a bad place after all. If he'd kept looking, he'd have seen a flashing lamp on a distant blue box, and heard the roar of ancient engines. But Ben was far too busy fitting in.

THE END

THE SHIP STREAKED THROUGH SPACE IN A BLAZE OF fire. The TARDIS scanner screen struggled to keep up.

'Well,' the Doctor said, tapping the image. 'There's your problem.'

'So let's do something about it,' Martha told him. 'Like, now.'

The Doctor sucked air noisily through his teeth. 'Not a lot we can do. Warp engines have got bonkers. That's a technical term,' he explained. 'Bonkers. Means, well – barmy. Mad. Bonkers, really. Ripping in and out of reality. The TARDIS could never get a fix. Can't land on it – even if we wanted to.'

'But they need help. They're sending out a distress signal. We can't just watch. What's going to happen to them?'

The Doctor worked the controls and the picture on the screen changed to show a planet hanging peacefully in space. 'Going to crash. Still on course, by the look of it. But they'll arrive with a bit more of a wallop than they intended. Wallop – '

'Is a technical term. I guessed.'

'Can't stop them crashing,' the Doctor admitted sadly. 'But we can get there before it happens. Lend a hand. Do what we can.'

'Is it a big ship?' Martha wondered. Seen against the blackness of space as it burned across the scanner it a impossible to tell.

'No. Tiny. Pilot and a few passengers. Half a dozen at most.'

'And where is it they're headed?'

The Doctor was already setting the TARDIS controls. 'Geravalon. Don't know it. Lots of swamps apparently. I'm aiming for a dry bit, but bring your wellies just in case.'

● ● ●

IN WHAT FELT LIKE AGES TO MARTHA BUT WAS actually no time at all, the TARDIS faded into existence on a muddy bank in the middle of a jungle. The crimson light of the two distant suns was filtering through the leaves of the enormous trees

Kiss of Life

WRITTEN BY
JUSTIN RICHARDS

ILLUSTRATIONS BY
ANDY WALKER

as Martha and the Doctor stepped from the TARDIS.

The Doctor jumped up and down on the muddy bank. 'Seems all right,' he decided. He pulled the door shut and patted the TARDIS affectionately. 'Don't go away,' he told it. 'Back in two shakes. Well, three shakes. Several shakes. Won't be long,' he finally decided.

'Which way?' Martha wanted to know. She found herself skidding down the bank as the Doctor strode purposefully into the jungle.

Then he swung round in a circle and headed back the other way. 'I was forgetting,' he said. 'Magnetic poles are reversed here, so north is south and south is north. Or maybe the other way round.'

'And where will the spaceship crash? North or south?'

'It'll be heading for the castle. But from the TARDIS estimates of its flight path, it'll overshoot and come down about half a mile this way.'

'Right.'

They walked on for several minutes in silence, slipping and sliding down banks and pushing through damp, twisted branches.

'Hang on, what castle?' Martha suddenly asked.

The Doctor didn't turn, he just pointed through a gap in the trees behind them. 'That one.'

Martha turned to look, and almost lost her footing. One foot splashed into a muddy puddle. But she hardly noticed. Through the trees she could see a massive castle towering above the jungle on a rocky hill. The crimson light of the sun picked out the stone battlements and the flag flying on the top of the tallest tower.

'Oh, right,' Martha said. 'That castle.'

'WHY HAVE WE STOPPED?' MARTHA ASKED A SHORT while later.

'Nearly there. But we don't want to be too close. If the ship comes down on top of us we'll be no help to anyone.'

'So we just have to wait for a crash?'

'That's about it,' the Doctor admitted. 'Mind you, it's worse for the people on board.'

The waiting reminded Martha of the hospital – waiting for an ambulance with an emergency that she knew was on its way. Knowing someone needed help, but for the moment powerless. In other circumstances, she thought, despite the damp swampy landscape, it would be quite beautiful.

As she looked round, she realised that something was watching her. Two small eyes peeping out from under a canopy of leaves. Martha gasped and took a step backwards, almost colliding with the Doctor.

He had seen it too. 'I don't think he means us any harm. Probably just curious. Aren't you?' he added, talking now to the creature hiding behind the leaves. He made some embarrassing 'coo-chi coo-chi coo' noises as he walked slowly towards it and pushed back the leaves.

Now she could see it, Martha didn't think the animal looked at all threatening. It was rather like a large lizard – about a metre and a half long, with pale green scaly skin that blended perfectly with the surrounding vegetation. But its face was almost human – with a bump of a nose and ridges that looked like eyebrows. Its eyes were round and at the front of the head, and its mouth was turned upwards as if it was smiling. As she got closer, Martha could see that it had a long tail, like a fish, dipping into a pool of water behind.

The Doctor was stroking the animal's head. 'Look at that,' he exclaimed. 'Like a chameleon.'

The lizard-creature's skin was changing colour as the Doctor stroked his hand across its head. It grew slowly pale, matching the Doctor. Martha laughed out loud to see that the animal's body was turning dark blue with pale lines down it – like the Doctor's suit.

'It'll get a quiff if you're not careful,' she joked.'

'You try.'

Martha patted the animal gently on the flank, and was surprised to find its body was warm. And after a moment, its skin darkened to a rich brown.

But then there was a breeze through the jungle, the noise of the ship coming down – a sudden roar of sound. The animal slithered backwards into the water. Its forked, fish-scale tail broke the surface as it dived, and it was gone.

The Doctor was already running, following the trail of fire that blazed across the sky. There was a huge tearing, wrenching explosion from ahead of them, and soon they were running through the smoking trench that the crashing ship had ripped through the jungle.

The ship was lying on its side. It was blistered and burning. Martha could see at once that no one could have escaped alive.

'I'm sorry,' the Doctor said. 'There was nothing we could do.'

There was, however, an escape pod. It worked, the Doctor explained, rather like an ejector seat.

'Only useful once you're in the atmosphere. I guess this type of ship gets used like an aircraft as well.'

It was the sound of the girl's weeping that led Martha to it. The pod had come down just at the edge of the jungle. A man was badly injured, lying half in and half out of the small circular hatch. The young woman was doing her best to help him.

'Must have left it to the last moment,' the Doctor said, running to help.

'Let me.' Martha gently eased the woman aside. She was dressed in simple clothes, streaked and stained with blood, and she seemed to be in shock. But she had managed to use a torn section of the man's uniform to bind his wounds and staunch the bleeding. From a quick check, Martha saw that the blood seemed to have come from the man's wounds. The woman's hands were covered with it.

'That's good,' Martha told her, retying the makeshift bandage. 'I think he'll make it.' She smiled, hoping to comfort the poor girl who was shivering despite the warmth of the jungle. 'You did exactly the right thing. You've saved his life.'

'Nice uniform,' the Doctor commented. 'You don't get that just for piloting the ship. Wonder who he is.'

'He is Prince Rodrique,' a gruff voice announced. 'Heir to the premiership of the Majullion Confederation.'

An elderly, aristocratic man was striding through the scarred jungle towards them. Behind him people were running with stretchers and what Martha guessed were medical kits. The aristocratic man waved for them to take over from Martha.

'You were on the Striker?' the man asked.

'No,' the Doctor told him. 'We saw it was in trouble. Followed it down. Did what we could.'

'Thank you.'

'She was already here,' Martha said, pointing to the young woman. 'She did the real work.'

The man turned and nodded curtly to the woman. 'A servant,' he explained. 'Rodrique didn't seem to mind transporting them. Help for the kitchens.'

'How many were there on board?' the Doctor asked.

'Rodrique was flying. He'd have stayed at the controls as long as he could to try to save them. She was lucky. Doesn't seem injured.'

'She's in shock,' Martha said.

'How many?' the Doctor repeated.

'Several. Maybe half a dozen.' The man turned away. 'Just servants.'

'They're still people,' Martha said angrily. The man was talking to the medic treating Rodrique and seemed not to hear.

The Doctor knelt beside the trembling girl. 'What's your name?'

Her words trembled as much as the rest of her. 'Sastra.'

'And you're here to work in the kitchens?' Martha asked helping her to her feet.

Sastra collapsed to her knees, her face creasing with pain. Martha waved at one of the medics to bring a stretcher. 'She might be "just" a servant,' Martha told him. 'But she needs help.'

Before long the two survivors were being stretchered back to the castle.

'You'd better come too,' the elderly man told the Doctor and Martha. 'Rodrique will want to thank you for your help.'

THE MAN IN CHARGE WAS CALLED PADROS. THE
Doctor and Martha asked him about Rodrique and the castle as they made their way through the dense jungle.

Martha caught sight of several of the lizard-like creatures watching from the undergrowth. They seemed interested in the group as they headed back to the castle, but they made no move to approach and she doubted if anyone else noticed, they blended so well with their background.

The ship, Padros told them, had been bringing Rodrique to his official retreat on Garavalon.

'The castle?' Martha prompted.

'Built to the original specifications of all the ancient fortresses that defended the Hodranic Line,' Padros said proudly.

'Fancy,' the Doctor said. 'Bit of history and heritage as well as the beautiful sunsets, then.'

'More than that,' Padros told them. 'Away from the riots and the unrest, the heir elect can plan for the future. He has great plans.' Padros glanced over at where the unconscious Rodrique was being carried on his stretcher. 'I do not agree with all of them, I have to say. I am old and change does not come easily to old men.'

'Tell me about it,' the Doctor murmured.

'Giving in to the servile classes and accepting they have rights. Allowing them to vote.' He shook his head. 'But he is to be our leader. We must respect his ideas however impulsive and ill-considered they might seem.'

'They sound pretty good to me,' Martha told him.

'Ah, but you are young. When you are young, everything is new and exciting and you think you know best.'

'And when you're old, you know you do,' the Doctor grinned.

The castle was even larger and more impressive than Martha had thought. She and the Doctor were each given a sumptuous room to stay in, and Padros insisted they should not leave until Rodrique had recovered enough to thank them for their efforts.

'And Sastra?' Martha asked.

'Her legs seem to be getting better. She starts work in the kitchens this evening.'

'I bet her room isn't like this,' Martha said to the Doctor when Padros had gone.

'Let's go and see,' the Doctor suggested.

They eventually found Sastra's room, in the cellars of the castle not far from the kitchens. The servants were kept well away from the more important people. But maybe, Martha thought, Rodrique's reforms would change that.

Though actually, Sastra's room wasn't too bad. Two star rather than five star, but it seemed comfortable enough. There was a bed, a table and chair, a viewscreen that worked like a telly, and an ensuite bathroom.

Sastra was lying on the bed. She looked pale, but insisted she was feeling better. She still spoke hesitantly, and Martha guessed she wasn't used to conversing with what she considered to be her betters. She was still wearing a shapeless overall-type number, but it didn't disguise the fact that the girl was seriously beautiful, though she didn't seem to realise it herself.

After a brief and diffident chat, Sastra shuffled to the door to show them out. Her legs obviously still hurt, but she tried not to show the pain. 'I have to go to work in the kitchens soon,' she said. 'They are planning a big celebration tomorrow evening. When Rodrique is better.'

THERE WAS FOOD WAITING FOR THEM IN THEIR ROOMS.
A severe-looking woman told Martha that Padros had given orders that she and the Doctor were not to be disturbed after their ordeals. They were welcome to treat the place as their own and he would meet them for lunch the next day.

Martha had to admit she was feeling pretty tired, and she was looking forward to a good night's sleep in the enormous, luxurious bed. Even so, she was surprised to find when she woke next day that she'd missed breakfast and it was almost time for lunch.

There was a beautiful view from her room out over the jungle. She could just make out the rip through the trees where the ship had crashed, and was saddened at

the thought of those people they hadn't been able to save.

Remembering how he had looked hanging half in and half out of the escape pod, Martha was surprised when Rodrique joined her, the Doctor and Padros for lunch. The man looked a little pale, but he insisted that after a night on the most advanced medication machines he was looking forward to the masked ball that evening.

'You will come of course – both of you. I owe you so much.'

'Oh, love to,' the Doctor said. 'I like a good knees up. You should see my Fosbury Flop. Oh hang on,' he frowned, 'maybe that's something else. Forget that last bit.'

Martha was entranced by the prince's deep voice and handsome features. She guessed she was probably not the only one, and as they discussed the ball in more detail she discovered she was right.

'There are the usual rumours, sire,' Padros said.

The Doctor was at once interested. 'Rumours? That sounds a bit intriguing. Family skeleton maybe? I always say, if you have a family skeleton there's no point hiding it in the closet. Much better to invite it out for a dance.'

'Nothing so interesting, I'm afraid,' Rodrique said. 'The rumours are that I shall announce my engagement.'

'And will you?' Martha asked.

'Between you and me – it's unlikely.' He smiled. 'Oh, I'm spoiled for choice and that's a fact. Lady Delamere's daughters. The Electrix of Gothard.'

'Shocking woman,' the Doctor said quickly.

'Margery Moops. Though she's not a serious option.'

'Are any of them?' Padros asked, leaning forward with interest.

Rodrique shook his head. 'Trouble is, I don't actually like any of them. Call me old fashioned, but I intend to marry for love not politics.'

'Quite right too,' the Doctor told him.

A thought occurred to Martha. 'You have asked Sastra to the dance, haven't you?'

'Sastra?' Rodrique turned to Padros for an answer.

'Servant girl, from the ship.'

'Don't remember much about it, I'm afraid,' Rodrique admitted. 'Spent most of the time trying to get here in one piece.' He shook his head sadly. 'I was the lucky one.'

'One of the lucky ones,' Martha said. 'Sastra survived. She got you out of the escape pod and staunched the bleeding. She saved your life.'

This seemed to be news to Rodrique, which annoyed Martha. But the prince insisted that Sastra be invited – despite Padros's protests.

'I'll go and tell Sastra the good news,' Martha said when the meal was over.

'She will need to be properly attired,' Padros insisted. 'For our guests – for you – I can provide clothes. But not for a servant. If she arrives dressed inappropriately, she will be thrown out.'

Martha was outraged. 'Just because she works in the kitchens and isn't on the prince's list of possible fiancés.'

'Maybe she's got a nice frock she can wear,' the Doctor said.

'Oh yeah – salvaged from the crashed ship. Bit tatty, bit burned, but maybe it doesn't smell too much of smoke so she won't get chucked out.'

'Or maybe,' the Doctor went on, 'I've got something in the TARDIS that would do. At a pinch.'

But when Martha and the Doctor arrived at Sastra's room, all thoughts of getting her to the masked ball disappeared.

Sastra could hardly stand, let alone walk or dance. Her legs gave

way as she climbed off her bed, and her face was etched with the pain. When Martha told her why they had come, the girl managed a weak smile.

'He is such a handsome man,' she said wistfully. 'My legs hurt so much, but I would love to go to the ball.' She sighed, falling back on the bed in near despair.

'We could ask for a wheelchair,' the Doctor suggested. But he didn't sound hopeful.

'You get her something to wear,' Martha told him. 'I'll see if I can get some medical help. If they can sort out a dying prince they ought to be able to mend pins and needles.' It was obviously more than that, but she smiled at Sastra, hoping to raise the girl's spirits.

'So, you know the prince well?' Martha asked when the Doctor had gone.

'I have watched him, here in the castle, many times.'

'You've been here before then?'

Sastra was staring off into space, remembering the past. 'I don't think he ever noticed me though.'

'Well then you're definitely coming along tonight. He's looking for a bride, and you'll knock him for six.'

Sastra frowned. 'Is that good?'

Martha laughed. 'Better believe it.'

MARTHA WAS ANNOYED BUT NOT SURPRISED TO FIND that servants weren't entitled to medical treatment. She hadn't got

time to argue about it now, but after the ball she'd be giving them a good earful.

The Doctor, however, came up trumps and earned himself an impulsive hug from Martha when he returned. Not only did he bring a stunning crimson ball gown trimmed with white lace, but also a small plastic bottle of tablets.

'Painkillers,' he explained to Sastra. 'And a bit more besides. Should sort out your legs for a few hours. Get you there and back, but try much more than a gentle stroll and you'll know about it. I can only give you one dose,' he went on. 'Can't risk giving you too much. They're digital – talk directly to the nerves and endorphins and… stuff.'

'So what's that mean?' Martha asked.

'Means they don't wear off so much as just stop. When your time's up – the pain'll be back like that.' He clicked his fingers.

'Take them now,' Martha insisted. 'You can barely stand up.'

The Doctor checked the clock beside Sastra's bed. 'You've got two hours exactly for each tablet. That gives you till midnight. Make sure you're back here, and grit your teeth because if the pain is increasing, it'll be back with a vengeance.'

SASTRA LOOKED GORGEOUS IN HER CRIMSON DRESS and a plain red mask that covered her eyes. Martha reckoned she looked quite good herself in a gown provided by the severe-faced woman. She'd been given a mask painted to look like a cat.

The Doctor was wearing his usual suit, and had a small, plain black mask. He wasn't wearing it, but holding it up in front of his face on a stick. Since everyone had heard about the strange Doctor and his friend, they all knew who he was anyway.

But is was Sastra who was the real enigma. Martha sat with her for a while at the side of the enormous ballroom. Despite the tablets the Doctor had given her, the girl was still in too much pain to stand up for any length of time.

'It's so beautiful,' Sastra said. 'I never imagined.'

'You not been in here before?'

Sastra shook her head. Behind the mask, her eyes were wide with wonder. Couples in splendid clothes danced past as the orchestra played. People stopped to look at Sastra, and whispered to each other as they moved on.

The prince – the only unmasked guest, if you forgave the Doctor's effort – danced with a variety of ever more beautiful women. But Martha was amused to see that he looked bored. And that Sastra's eyes never strayed from him for long. The girl was smitten.

Despite sitting at the side of the room, Sastra had soon drawn a small crowd. No one knew who she was or where she had come from. More than the Doctor or Martha, Sastra was the mystery guest. She chatted and made small talk. She was witty and intelligent – none of these stuffy people would ever guess she was just a servant, Martha thought.

And eventually – inevitably – Prince Rodrique came to see who was attracting such interest.

Sastra was suddenly quiet as the handsome Rodrique pushed through the group of people. He was as handsome as Sastra was beautiful, and it seemed she was as clever and amusing as he was.

'I thought I knew everyone here,' Rodrique said. 'But you are a stranger – a beautiful stranger – in our midst. You are new to our castle?'

She nodded nervously.

'Then the very least I can do to make you welcome is to invite you to dance.'

Sastra looked up at Rodrique as he offered her his hand. There was an impulsive smattering of applause from nearby. A woman who had just danced with the prince turned away in undisguised jealousy.

'She's rather tired,' Martha told Rodrique. 'Her legs are very weak.'

But Sastra got slowly to her feet. 'I would be honoured and delighted,' she said.

The Doctor danced with Martha. He had put his mask down, all pretence at pretence now abandoned. 'They make a lovely couple,' he said as they spun past the happy prince and his beautiful partner.

But as they passed, Martha caught a glimpse behind Sastra's mask. She saw the tears of pain streaming down the girl's face and the frown of agony.

Then the clock began to strike.

'Oops,' the Doctor said, letting go of Martha.

At the same moment, Sastra pulled away from the prince. She gathered her long ballgown in her hands and stumbled from the room as the guests looked on in astonishment and the music faded to the chimes of midnight.

Rodrique ran after Sastra. Martha and the Doctor were close behind. They found him half way down the magnificent staircase that led to the entrance hall on the floor below. He was holding one of Sastra's shoes.

'She never even told me her name,' Rodrique said. 'But I could see her beauty despite the mask. And already I have lost her.' He stood up, lifting the delicate shoe high above his head so everyone could see. 'But I shall find her. Whoever this shoe fits…'

The Doctor interrupted him. 'Don't be daft, Prince Charming,' he said. 'It was Sastra. And if I'm right, we need to find her – before it's too late.'

'She'll have gone back to her room,' Martha said.

'If she managed to get there.' The Doctor was grave. 'I only just realised, while I was watching her dance, that there's more to this than we thought.'

'When she was on the ship, Rodrique – when she saved your life…' Martha began.

'I am grateful for that!' the Prince interrupted.

'I know, but her legs…' Martha began to explain, hoping that at last the poor girl could be treated properly.

'She is ill?'

'Oh that's only the half of it,' the Doctor said. 'Come on!'

SASTRA WAS NOT IN HER ROOM, AND RODRIQUE ordered a search of the castle.

'I hope she's not tried to go back outside,' the Doctor said.

'Why would she do that?' Martha asked.

The Doctor didn't answer. While Padros organised the search, he led Martha and Rodrique back towards the ballroom.

'There is a quicker way,' Rodrique pointed out.

'But this is more private. Less well lit. Shadowy and unwalked…'

'So why would she come this way?' Martha asked. 'She needs help.'

'She doesn't want any help. She doesn't want anyone to see what's happening to her.'

As he spoke, he stepped to one side in the dimly-lit corridor, and Martha saw that what she had thought was a shadow was actually a body lying on the floor.

'Sastra!' Martha ran to her, feeling at once for a pulse in her neck.

The girl's skin was rough and damp and warm. As Rodrique lifted one of the glowing lamps from the wall nearby and brought it over, Martha saw that Sastra's skin seemed to be lined and ridged. Her legs were sticking out of the crimson gown. They were swollen and covered in scales. As Martha watched, the legs seemed to grow together – into a single scaly limb. The feet were angled apart. Like a forked tail.

The Doctor knelt beside Martha. 'We may be too late,' he said sadly. 'If only I'd realised sooner.'

'What's happened to her?' Martha asked.

'Some sort of infection?' Rodrique suggested. He set down the lamp and knelt beside Sastra, taking one of her scaly hands between his own. 'What can we do?'

'She's dying,' the Doctor said. 'It was your blood that made her change. She probably licked your wounds when she first found you, trying desperately to help. So much more powerful than just a touch which might colour the skin.'

Martha gave a gasp of astonishment. 'You mean – she's really one of those lizard things from the jungle?'

'She absorbed human DNA, a genetic imprint,' the Doctor said. 'Her body is trying to change back, without more genetic material it's trying to revert, but she's changed too much and she can't.'

'What can we do?' Rodrique looking imploringly at the Doctor. 'I can't lose her now. There must be something.'

'Can't we get her more genetic material?' Martha said.

The Doctor shook his head. 'Would have to be from the same source. And touch isn't enough. She'd have to, I don't know…' He leaped to his feet and snapped his fingers. 'Of course. She'd have to get a direct infusion of…'

But Rodrique was not listening. He gave a sudden hopeless sob of anguish, leaned forward, and kissed Sastra on her near-lifeless lips.

For a moment, there was no response, but then she was kissing him back.

'Yeah,' the Doctor said. 'That ought to do the trick.'

Martha stared at him. 'Transferring genetic information in saliva? From a kiss?'

'It's worked before,' he reminded her.

Beside them, Rodrique rose slowly to his feet, helping up the beautiful woman he had been kissing – Sastra. Arm in arm they walked slowly back to the ballroom, the Doctor and Martha forgotten in the aura of their love.

◄●●►

'SHOULD WE JUST SLIP AWAY LIKE this?' Martha wondered.

'Oh I hate goodbyes.'

Martha's foot had sunk deep into a muddy pool. 'I hate swamps. Even when I'm dressed for it.'

'I said to bring your wellies.'

Martha struggled onwards in her ball gown. The hem was plastered in mud and there was a rip in the side where a branch had caught it.

'It's this way,' the Doctor told her. 'Not far now.'

'Even though north is south and south is north?'

'Oh yeah. Wouldn't forget that, would I?' He swung round. 'As I said – TARDIS is this way. And a bit of a trek, I'm afraid.'

'Typical. Terrific. Thanks.'

'Oh please, don't mention it.'

'So will Sastra be all right now? I mean, is she completely human?'

'Is anyone?' the Doctor wondered. 'Her legs will always be a bit painful. The ache of something she's not supposed to have. But yeah – she'll be fine. Well, just so long as she gets her genetic infusion every, what, 24 hours or so?'

'A kiss?'

'A kiss. Rodrique's kiss, it's his imprint that she needs.'

'He has to kiss her every day,' Martha realised.

'Yuk,' the Doctor said with a sniff.

'Or else she'll die. Die for lack of love.'

'Afraid so.'

'That's…' Martha hesitated. She wasn't sure what it was. Maybe it was romantic. Maybe it wasn't.

'Sweet,' the Doctor finished for her. 'And sad.'

They reached the top of a muddy bank, and Martha could see the TARDIS standing a little way in front of them, bathed in the crimson light of the early dawn. But the Doctor was looking back the way had come.

'Sad and sweet,' he murmured.

Martha turned to see what he was looking at. In the distance, the castle was silhouetted against the rising suns. Pale light spilled from one large window, and in it – black on yellow – Martha could see two figures. A man and a woman. They were dancing, holding each other close, tight, in love.

What Martha could not see was that the woman was crying again. But now they were tears of joy as well as pain.

THE END

THE DOCTOR STEPPED AWAY FROM THE CONTROLS and folded his arms. 'Well?'

Martha looked up. 'Gravity normal… atmosphere breathable.'

'Bingo! Top marks, Martha Jones. Seriously, I'm impressed. Fresh air's a bit tricky to find when you're this far out.'

'How far out are we exactly?'

'Well, the TARDIS doesn't really do 'exactly'. But I'd say we're pretty far out, wouldn't you?'

Martha grinned and flipped the door control. 'What are we waiting for then?' She turned on her heel and strode down the ramp – and gasped as she stepped through the doors into paradise.

The TARDIS was underwater. Above Martha's head, shafts of light from an unseen sky bobbed and danced down through a blue-green ocean. All around her were the spectacular colours of an immense coral reef, thrusting from the seabed in a tangled forest writhing with life: scuttling shrimps, sinuous eels, sea anemones swaying with the ebb and flow of the ocean, and hundreds – no, thousands – of brightly jewelled fish, twisting together in shimmering shoals in the open water, and darting in ones and twos between the coral outcrops. Martha instinctively held her breath, not quite understanding why her lungs hadn't filled with water, before her mind caught up with her senses and she realised that somewhere in front of her there must be a barrier holding the ocean at bay. As she gazed out into the impenetrable blue distance, a pair of dolphins appeared through the deep and came undulating towards her, bobbing down to inspect the new arrivals with keen curiosity. Martha walked up to them and stretched out a hand. Her fingertips made contact with an impossibly smooth and perfectly invisible surface, no more than a few millimetres thick. On the other side, the dolphins nuzzled eagerly at her outstretched fingers.

'Doctor,' she breathed. 'It's…'

'Certainly is,' murmured the Doctor as he locked the TARDIS and joined her. 'And now it definitely qualifies as far out. On the list of things I was expecting to find out here, this ranks somewhere in the low billions.'

'We went to the aquarium in Brighton once,' said Martha, as the dolphins turned tail and butterflied away into the deep. 'Wasn't as good as this.'

'Think you'll find we're the ones in the fish tank here,' observed the Doctor. 'It's a big old biome

Deep Wa

by the looks of it.'

'Like an underwater base?'

'That sort of thing, yeah. But on a massive scale. A huge reinforced bump on the bottom of the ocean. Like the Millennium Dome, only a thousand times bigger.'

'And a million times more useful?'

'Definitely.'

Martha looked down at her feet. They were standing on a floor of brushed steel. As she took in her surroundings she realised that the Doctor was right: the TARDIS had materialised near the edge of a colossal dome that rose invisibly around them, arching over their heads to reach its apex at some unimaginable distance above. She could barely guess at its size, but where it met the floor there was no discernible curve. Far off to her left – perhaps three quarters of a mile away – she could dimly make out an enormous inner wall, a metal bulkhead that followed the upward sweep of the dome and blocked off the view beyond, presumably leading on to another chamber in this underwater world. To the right, this time only a couple of hundred metres away, was another. 'So we're inside a kind of… segment in the dome,' she deduced.

'That's it. A slice of the cake, if you like.'

'So what is it? A scientific base?'

'On this scale, I reckon it's more likely to be a city. Take a look behind you.'

Martha turned and caught her breath for a second time. She'd been so entranced by the view outside the dome that she hadn't registered what was behind them. Beyond the TARDIS lay an even more awesome sight: a vast interior space bristling with towers of glass, concrete and steel, skyscrapers stretching up forty, fifty storeys, connected to one another by walkways and tunnels, through which she could see gleaming silver tube-trains silently whisking their occupants to and fro. It reminded her of nothing so much as the Manhattan skyline – only here there was no sky. Just the steel bulkheads, the invisible dome, and above it the turquoise ocean, shedding ever-changing beams of dappled light across the city.

'And this is just one segment…' she whispered. 'Have you ever seen anything like it?'

'Not out here I haven't,' the Doctor replied.

'Oh, hello. You've got that serious thing going on,' said Martha. 'That Something's Wrong voice.'

'No, it's just …' murmured the Doctor. 'I dunno. We'll see.' His voice lightened. 'Shall we explore?'

'Thought you'd never ask.'

THE DOCTOR RETURNED FROM THE TILL, GRINNING as he pocketed his psychic paper. 'It's okay,' he whispered, 'He's convinced I'm an old mate from school and he insisted the bill was on the house.'

Martha looked over to the beaming proprietor and returned his

WRITTEN BY **NICHOLAS PEGG**
ILLUSTRATIONS BY **BRIAN WILLIAMSON**

wave. 'Just as well,' she hissed, 'since we don't even know what sort of money they use here. Okay – where next?'

They'd been in the underwater city for a couple of hours, during which they'd indulged in a spot of window-shopping, found a library, a hospital and a school, and wandered through a park where, on fresh-smelling grass nourished by artificial sunlight, a gang of children noisily played a game not quite like football. Finally they'd ended up in a café, where they'd enjoyed a slice of something not quite like carrot cake and a cup of something not quite like coffee.

'We haven't been up any of these towers yet,' said the Doctor as they stepped out into the street. 'Bet the view's good.'

'The view's good everywhere!' retorted Martha, gazing up for the hundredth time at the teeming tropical seascape that hung over every boulevard, square and alleyway.

'How about we take a lift up there?' suggested the Doctor, pointing up to a huge horizontal tube a hundred metres long that was slung like a hammock between the floors of two of the tallest skyscrapers, dotted with windows on three levels like the fuselage of an airliner.

'As long as it's not like the Empire State Building,' muttered Martha, but the Doctor was already striding towards the nearest transport kiosk, and she had to run to catch up.

MARTHA HAD BEEN EXPECTING A PONDEROUS
industrial lift like the ones at Goodge Street station, but instead she and the Doctor were shown into a sleek, windowless capsule built for two. It was one of a rank of fifty or more – some equipped to travel vertically, others horizontally, and some even diagonally – that lined the walls of a terminus patrolled by sleek, efficient and impeccably polite robots who hovered an inch above the ground as they glided silently about their business. As the lift door hissed shut on the teeming lobby, Martha studied the illuminated display, a column of numbers from 1 to 60.

'Pick a number, any number,' encouraged the Doctor.

Martha shrugged. 'Twenty-two?'

'Two little ducks...' The Doctor flicked his finger over the number 22. It lit up green, and instantly Martha felt the lift begin to rise with heart-stopping speed. Beneath the green 22, the other numbers flickered upwards in red, and then stopped at 21. The illuminated 22 went dark. The 21 turned green.

'Hello,' Martha grinned. 'I knew nothing could be perfect – not even this place. The lift's on the blink.' She copied the Doctor's movement of a moment before, passing her finger over the number 22. It changed to red for an instant, and then went dark. The 21 remained stubbornly green.

'Hmm,' hmmed the Doctor. He reached out and flicked the 23. Instantly Martha felt the lift make the short trip between the two floors. The lights changed accordingly: the number 23 turned green. Then the Doctor tried 22 again. Once more, it flickered red and went out.

'Now that's interesting,' said the Doctor. 'A floor that doesn't want to be visited.'

'Could just be closed for maintenance,' suggested Martha.

'Nah, I don't think so,' said the Doctor. 'Every time we press 22, someone's overriding the circuit, fast as lightning.' He was already pointing his sonic screwdriver at the control panel. 'In fact it's just a little bit frightening. But with a touch of expert timing, I can override the overrider...' He flicked 22 and instantly activated the screwdriver in three short bursts. 'Et... *voilà*!' The number 22 turned green and the door swished open. 'C'mon, quick,' said the Doctor. 'And keep your eyes peeled. Looks like someone's going to a lot of trouble to stop people getting off at this floor.'

They emerged on one side of a dimly lit passageway. A row of doors, each with a porthole-like window, ran along the opposite wall. As Martha looked up and down the corridor, she realised that they were quite alone. There was none of the bustle she'd seen elsewhere in the city. She crossed the corridor and peered through the window in the nearest door. On the other side was a small room, empty apart from a computer terminal on the far wall. The view through the next window was the same. She idly flicked a finger over the entry light and the door swished open. 'Not much going on here,' she called back to the Doctor, flicking the door closed again. She moved on to look through the third window and stifled a scream.

The room was like all the others, but this time there was a man inside. And he was in trouble. He was stumbling drunkenly around the enclosed space, clawing furiously at his neck. His face was bathed in sweat, the veins throbbing at his temples, and his breath came in ragged gasps. He saw Martha through the window, and for an instant his eyes lit up with something like hope. Without hesitating, Martha flicked the entry light. Nothing happened. As the man staggered towards the window she could see with horrible clarity the fear that was consuming him.

'Doctor!' she called, but he was already by her side. Together they struggled to open the door, but the controls refused to respond. Beside the window was a small, neat red label marked 'Terminal 236'. Beneath it a display reading 'NO ENTRY' flashed on and off remorselessly. Inside the room, the man was scrabbling pathetically at the window, tears pouring down his face, his eyes staring imploringly into Martha's. She could hear his hoarse, rapid breathing, and could see that he was growing weaker by the second, his eyes clouding over as if, even in his frenzied terror, he was battling to resist falling asleep. 'Hold on!' Martha yelled, 'We'll get you out!' But she already knew it was hopeless. The Doctor was frantically trying out different settings on his sonic screwdriver, but the door refused to budge. Martha knew that the man behind it was dying. She looked away in horror as, gasping and gulping like a drowning man, he slumped forward. His cheek squashed grotesquely against the window, leaving a smear of sweat and spittle as he slid down the door and out of sight. With a final

ghastly rattle, the breathing stopped.

The Doctor gently lowered the sonic screwdriver. For a moment, neither of them said anything. Martha looked up at him and was about to open her mouth when the 'NO ENTRY' sign stopped flashing and blinked out. At the same instant the door controls flickered into life.

'It's all back to normal,' breathed Martha. The Doctor moved to operate the door control, but she grabbed his wrist. 'Wait,' she said. 'There's some sort of gas in there.'

'Oh, I don't think so,' said the Doctor grimly. 'Not any more.'

He pulled free and flicked his hand over the light.

The door hissed open and the dead man slumped out into the corridor. Martha shuddered as she saw the terror in his staring eyes. She knelt down and checked for a pulse she knew she wouldn't find, and then pulled his lower lip down with her thumb, peering at the gums beneath before gently closing the man's eyes.

'What's the verdict?' asked the Doctor.

'His mucous membranes are unnaturally pink,' said Martha. 'So are his lips. And he was hyperventilating. Looks exactly like carbon monoxide poisoning.'

'Something like that,' agreed the Doctor.

'Reminds me of a bloke we got in A&E just after Christmas. They pulled him out of his garage in time, but he was all pink like this.' She drew a wallet from the dead man's pocket and flipped it open. 'His name's Leonard Farnham.' Tucked beside the calling-card was a photo of the man being hugged by two laughing children. Martha slipped the wallet back into the man's pocket. 'So someone locked him in this room, pumped it full of gas, then sucked it back out again as soon as he was dead?'

The Doctor nodded darkly and crossed to the computer terminal that stood against the far wall of the room. The screen was blank. He tapped a few keys.

'What was he working on?' asked Martha.

'No idea. Whatever it was, it's been erased. The drive's empty. Blank screen.'

Martha straightened up. 'What do we do now?'

'I think we'd better find out who's in charge of the air conditioning around here, don't you?'

'And how do we do that?'

'Absolutely no idea.'

'Wait a minute,' said Martha. 'I thought you said the screen was blank.'

'It is.'

'So what's that?'

The Doctor followed her finger. A cursor had just finished racing across the computer screen. In clear, no-nonsense capitals, it said 'GET IN THE LIFT'.

Martha swallowed. 'Someone knows we're here.'

'Looks that way.' The Doctor cast his eyes around the room.

'Do we ignore it?'

'If he's got his free hand on the gas taps, that might not be a very clever idea.'

The cursor raced across the screen. 'CORRECT. GET IN THE LIFT.'

'Well, seeing as you put it like that,' said the Doctor, twirling the sonic screwdriver in one hand and tapping absent-mindedly on the computer keyboard with the other, 'Let's get in the lift. Come on.' Pocketing the sonic screwdriver, he strode out of the room and back across the corridor. Martha followed him nervously.

Two robots had appeared in the corridor, silently flanking the open door of the lift. As the Doctor and Martha stepped past them into the capsule, the robots glided across the passage towards the corpse of Leonard Farnham. Martha turned and caught a glimpse of metallic cables whipping out from concealed apertures, lifting the body clear of the ground. Then the lift doors hissed shut. She turned to the Doctor. 'I suppose by the time this floor's available again,

there'll be no trace he was ever here.'

'I should think that's the idea,' replied the Doctor quietly.

THERE WAS A SOFT HUM AND MARTHA FELT THE LIFT moving up – or was it down? No lights appeared on the display to tell them where they were going this time. Martha looked up at the Doctor. His face was set.

After a few moments the lift came to rest and the doors swished open. They emerged into a large, elegantly furnished chamber dominated by a rectangular window the size of a small cinema screen, through which the now familiar sight of the ocean shimmered and undulated in all its infinite variety. In the centre of the room was a huge oval desk inlaid with buttons and viewing screens, and behind the desk sat a man who was staring at them with an expression that Martha couldn't quite decipher. It was either fascination or fury.

He was old, very old, and everything from the straggly white hair to the deep furrows in his gaunt face spoke of exhaustion

and decrepitude. Everything, that is, apart from the glint of determination in his watery eyes. The old man regarded them solemnly, and after a moment his dry lips opened. Without any other discernible movement, he spoke.

'Welcome.'

'Welcome to where?' asked the Doctor evenly. Martha glanced at him. His face was almost as impassive as that of their host.

'You are in Subaqua One.'

'As underwater names go, that has to be just about the lamest I've heard,' said the Doctor rudely. 'Let me guess – this planet is a colony. You've terraformed it and now you're branching out into seabases. And you're in charge of this one. How am I doing?'

'Remarkably well,' said the man. 'I am indeed the controller of Subaqua One. This facility is the first of its kind on the planet Miletus. Entirely self-sustaining. Down here we have everything we need.'

'And you've got such a lovely view,' added the Doctor. 'I expect you never tire of looking at it.'

The controller regarded him levelly.

'Of course, if you did ever tire of it,' continued the Doctor recklessly, 'I suppose you could always do something like this.' Without warning he strode up to the desk and plunged his sonic screwdriver into a terminal. Instantly the view through the window shimmered, dissolved, blurred, and reshaped itself into...

'London!' cried Martha. They were no longer underwater. The ocean had been replaced by the unmistakeable skyline of Martha's home city. Big Ben, the London Eye, St Paul's Cathedral...

'Or how about this?' the Doctor twisted the sonic screwdriver again, and the view dissolved once more, reassembling itself into stars, planets, the whorl of a spiral galaxy, a breathtaking vista of deep space. 'Or maybe...' he twisted it again, and this time the view coalesced into a vision of hell.

Martha shuddered. Through the window was a ravaged, blackened wasteland swirling with storms. Dust and ashes blew fitfully through the skeletal remains of long-ruined buildings. Martha had never seen such a dead, forsaken place. She looked away. 'I don't like that one, Doctor. Choose something nicer.'

'I don't think so,' said the Doctor softly. 'You see, that's the real outside.' His voice grew colder as he turned to the man behind the desk. 'Isn't it?'

'What have you done?' The controller was staring at the screen and quivering with horror. 'You mustn't...'

'Don't worry,' said the Doctor, his voice becoming gentler. 'It's only your viewing screen. Everywhere else in this brainwashed utopia of yours they're still seeing the ocean.'

Martha stared at him. 'You mean – they don't know?'

'That's right,' said the Doctor. 'Nobody knows. Nobody except him. That's true, isn't it?'

The controller's steely resolve seemed to have deserted him. His head fell into his hands, and for a moment Martha thought he was actually weeping. She looked up again at the terrible devastation through the viewing screen. 'What happened here?'

'War,' said the controller simply, raising his tired old head. 'A terrible, stupid war.'

'That's the usual kind,' murmured the Doctor.

'But how come nobody knows?' demanded Martha. 'The guy in the café, he said his parents came from another planet… Sarpy-something.'

'Sarpedon.'

The Doctor leaned over the desk. 'That was one of the old Earth outposts, wasn't it? Last time I heard, it was getting pretty overcrowded.'

The controller looked up at him and frowned. 'Your information is accurate, if a little out of date,' he said pettishly. 'Sarpedon was desperately overpopulated. But Miletus was the jewel in our colonial crown. So when war started looking more and more likely at home, our government appointed a taskforce to build this place. Utterly self-sufficient, utterly resistant to firepower, utterly sealed off from the outside world. It nearly bankrupted them. And when it was ready, they transmatted the first inhabitants in from the other side of the world.'

MARTHA WAS BEGINNING TO GRASP THE SHEER magnitude of what the old man was saying. 'So they believed all along that this place was under the sea?'

'With a very few exceptions, yes, they did. The infrastructure was established first. Teachers, doctors, farmers,' – the man gestured to himself without a trace of pride – 'scientists.'

'But war came sooner than you expected.' The Doctor was leaning over the desk, a look of intense interest in his eyes.

The old man nodded wearily. 'The government never had the chance to relocate here. They'd barely received the news that Sarpedon was destroyed before the bombardment began here.' He looked out of the window on the blasted

landscape. 'Seven hours. That's all it took. I stood here and watched it happen. I was a junior telegraphist at the time.'

'Junior?' said Martha, looking askance at the frail old man. 'Just how long ago was this?'

The controller turned and regarded her with infinite sadness. 'Sixty-eight years.'

Martha swallowed. 'So if you were a junior,' continued the Doctor as she absorbed this latest shock, 'whose decision was it to keep the illusion going? To fool these people into thinking that the war never happened?'

'My superior. The head of the science division,' said the controller. 'He died nearly forty years ago. They're all dead now. I'm the last.'

'The last one who knows the truth?'

'Yes, Doctor.'

'And what happens when you die?'

'Nothing. For more than sixty years, my late colleagues and I have been refining and developing the technology in anticipation of the day when it becomes self-perpetuating. We're only the smallest step away from total automation. My robots will carry on the work here. My task is all but completed.'

'But the dolphins!' cried Martha suddenly. 'When we first landed. Those dolphins were real. They saw me. They swam up to me!'

'Psycho-cognitive interaction,' said the man with an airy wave of his hand. 'That was one of our very earliest refinements. We perfected it soon after the war. Your

subconscious mind manipulates the images and you interact with them as you expect you should. It all helps to preserve the illusion. It's a very simple technique really.'

'And you're telling me that in sixty-eight years, nobody's ever shown the slightest interest in leaving this city, in going up to the surface, not even for a holiday?' demanded the Doctor. 'Hasn't anybody ever asked why their relatives never write to them?'

'Oh, but their relatives do write to them,' said the man. 'People regularly receive holo-messages from the surface, and from the home planet too.'

'Fabricated by you?'

'With a little help from their own subliminal yearnings. And yes, when people want to leave Subaqua One for a break on the surface, they do.'

For the first time, the Doctor looked baffled. 'How?'

'I worked on that project myself as a youngster. Suppose one of our citizens wants to visit his family for a fortnight. He buys his ticket. Having entered the automated travel terminus, he passes through a chamber that puts him into a coma. Quite painlessly and quite harmlessly, I assure you. The robots take him to the vivarium, and for a fortnight he lies safely locked away from prying eyes, suspended in sleep and fed with nutrients. And at the end of the fortnight he arrives back in the travel terminus, healthy and refreshed, full of happy memories of his holiday above the waves.'

'False memories, implanted by you,' growled the Doctor. 'What you're doing is disgusting.'

'It was a sound political decision to optimise the predicted survival chances of our species, Doctor,' said the controller coldly, his face suddenly stern. 'Don't you see, if these people knew the truth, they'd have nothing to live for. Their lives would have no meaning. Their home planet is destroyed, their families are dead, and outside this dome there's nothing but a poisoned wilderness. If they knew that, our society would collapse within hours. There'd be desperation, chaos, lawlessness. As it is, we have almost no crime here. We have full employment. We have a clean, safe city. These people are happy. They live complete lives. They're full of optimism for the future. It's a perfect system.'

'Only it's not perfect, is it?' said the Doctor angrily. 'Leonard Farnham could tell you that.'

'Who?'

'The man you just murdered.' The old man winced at the word. 'Found something out, didn't he?'

The controller sighed. 'Every once in a while, somebody does. Either the conditioning doesn't quite work, or else a programmer comes across something in the mainframe and puts two and two together…'

'And for that, you murder them in cold blood? You poison their air-conditioning? You kill people just to preserve the lie that keeps this place going?' Martha had never seen the Doctor so angry. 'And what are you going to tell *his* family? That he's gone on another holiday?'

'Something like that,' said the controller dismissively.

'Why didn't you just lock us up and gas us too?' demanded Martha. 'What's with the invitation to get in the lift?'

'You're strangers,' said the controller. 'I had to know why you

were here, and how that box of yours penetrated the dome.'

The Doctor looked up from studying the controls on the desk. 'So you've been watching us then?'

'Of course. And you, Doctor, were suspicious from the very start. Why?'

'Well, it's obvious, isn't it?' cried the Doctor. 'Bottle-nose dolphins, staghorn coral, manta rays, seahorses, leatherback turtles? It's like *Finding Nemo* out there. Terraforming is one thing, but an entire ecosystem that belongs to an extinct planet on the other side of the galaxy? That's just bonkers.'

The controller smiled thinly. 'Ah. You're clearly more knowledgeable about such things than anyone here, Doctor. One of my predecessors was something of a historian. I believe he found the images in an old archive somewhere. So they come from Earth, do they?'

'Yes, they come from Earth,' said the Doctor fiercely. 'And so do you. So do all these people. The Earth might have been dead for tens of thousands of years, but you're still human beings.' The Doctor cast his eyes around the room despairingly. 'Look what you've done to yourselves.'

'Don't judge us too harshly, Doctor,' said the controller. 'I can't easily tell you what a burden it has been keeping the secret all these years.'

'Then why keep it?' shouted the Doctor. 'Look at yourself. Look at all the – the *trouble* you've gone to – and for what? This isn't living. Human beings are resourceful, inventive, clever. They're survivors. They respond to adversity. That's what they do best. You've got hospitals here, you've got schools, universities, laboratories, theatres, libraries. Hasn't it ever occurred to you that these people could make something of this planet of yours? They could be out there right now, working out how to clean the air, how to grow crops, how to build new cities, instead of floating around in here like zombies.'

'So what do you suggest?' asked the controller bitterly. 'What should I do?'

'Open their eyes,' said the Doctor simply. 'Switch off this illusion. Tell them the truth.'

'I can't do that,' said the controller. 'I just can't.'

A tremulous voice came from behind them. 'Maybe you can't – but I can.'

The Doctor and Martha whirled around. Standing in the doorway was a boy, no older than fourteen or fifteen. Martha

couldn't help thinking she'd seen him somewhere before. In his trembling hands he held a compact and oddly shaped gun, which was pointing directly at the old man behind the desk. The boy's soft, handsome features were set in a mask of pain and anger.

'How did you get in here?' The controller seemed more astonished than alarmed.

'Ah, that'd be me, I'm afraid,' said the Doctor apologetically. 'The sonic screwdriver's a useful gadget. I locked off the message you sent to the computer terminal. You remember, the one that told us to get in the lift. And then I sent the lift back down.' He turned to the boy. 'I thought your father might have appreciated someone carrying on the trail he left for you.'

'His father!' whispered Martha. Suddenly she remembered the photo in the dead man's wallet. She looked at the boy tenderly. 'What's your name?'

'Dan.' The boy's eyes hadn't left the old man behind the desk, who was now staring at him with something like fear. 'How long have you been lurking in the doorway?' demanded the controller.

The boy's lip trembled. 'Long enough,' he whispered, and fired the gun.

THERE WAS NO BANG – JUST A WHOOSH OF AIR AND THE old man slumped over the desk in a heap. Martha ran to his side.

'Don't worry, he's not dead,' said the boy. 'He deserves to be, but I'm not like him. Not a killer. And neither was my dad.'

'Your dad told you about his suspicions?' asked the Doctor.

'Yeah. Last night. He said he was going to hack into the mainframe at two o'clock today and find out for sure. And if I didn't hear from him by half past, I should go to Terminal 236.' The boy's voice was wavering again as he threw the gun to the floor. 'He gave me that.'

'Your father was a seeker of the truth,' said the Doctor gently. 'There's no braver kind of man.'

Silently, and with a curious dignity, the boy began to cry. Martha crossed to him and put her arm around his shoulder. 'He'd be proud of you.'

'We had a brilliant holiday last year,' the boy gulped between sobs. 'Me and my parents, and my brother. On the surface. The beach was amazing. And … none of it was true.'

Martha didn't know what to say, but she instinctively tightened her grip on the slight shoulders. The boy looked up at her and, after a couple of sniffs, managed to regain his composure. 'Who are you?' he asked.

'Just visitors.'

'What are you gonna do now, Dan?' asked the Doctor quietly.

Dan looked around the control room and swallowed hard. 'I'm going to do what you said,' he replied. 'I'm going to end this stupid lie.'

'What about him?' Martha nodded to the old man, still slumped lifelessly across the desk.

'He'll sleep for the next twelve hours. When he wakes up he'll be in a police cell. My mum's a magistrate.'

'Make sure he's treated fairly,' said the Doctor. He flipped open a glass panel and studied it for a moment before tapping out a series of codes on the concealed keys. Then he beckoned Dan over and pointed to a small grey switch.

'That's the one you want,' said the Doctor. 'Flick that and it's all out in the open. No more city beneath the sea. The whole dome will see what's really out there.'

'Thank you,' said the boy.

'It's going to be very tough,' said the Doctor. 'You'll have to be strong. You and your family. And your children, one day.'

'I know,' said Dan. 'But what matters is the truth.'

'I'm glad you think that,' said the Doctor. 'Because you're right. Good luck, Dan.' He reached out and clasped the boy's hand in his.

Dan looked up at him. 'You're going?'

'It's time,' said the Doctor.

'Doctor, we can't leave him to do this,' protested Martha. 'He's only a kid!'

'So were you, once,' said the Doctor. 'And so was I. He'll be fine. Won't you, Dan?'

'Sure,' the boy smiled. He extended his hand to Martha, and she shook it. 'Take care.'

'You too.'

The Doctor turned and strolled towards the lift. Martha followed. As they reached the doorway, she touched his arm. 'It's just so awful,' she whispered. 'It's going to be terrible for them to find out.'

'It's real life, Martha,' said the Doctor softly. 'Nobody ever said it was going to be easy.'

Martha looked back across the room to Dan, standing small beneath the huge viewing screen. The boy glanced back at them and smiled sadly, bravely. Then he reached down and flicked the switch.

THE END